PIG PARK

PIG PARK

CINCO PUNTOS PRESS
www.cincopuntos.com

Claudia Guadalupe Martínez

FIRST EDITION
10 9 8 7 6 5 4 3 2 1

Library of Congress Cataloging-in-Publication Data

Martinez, Claudia Guadalupe, 1978-
  Pig Park / by Claudia Guadalupe Martinez. — First edition.
    pages cm

ISBN 978-1-935955-76-4 (hardback); ISBN 978-1-935955-77-1 (paperback); ISBN 978-1-935955-78-8 (Ebook)
  [1. Neighborhoods—Fiction. 2. Community life—Illinois—Chicago—Fiction. 3. Bakers and bakeries—Fiction. 4. Family life—Illinois—Chicago—Fiction. 5. Building—Fiction. 6. Hispanic Americans—Fiction. 7. Chicago (Ill.)—Fiction.] I. Title.

PZ7.M36714Pig 2014
[Fic]—dc23
                                    2013040645

Cover and book design by Sergio Gomez
The year of babies!
And the internship of Stephanie Amerena and Amber James.

When I told my father I wanted to write
a book, he said I should write two, three
or more. This book is in memory of him,
for encouraging big dreams.

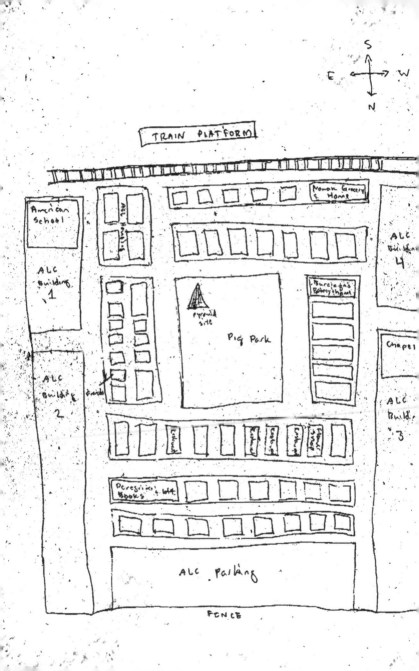

"So a bunch of us want to hang out, build a pyramid in the middle of Pig Park and save our neighborhood. Are you in?"

CHAPTER 1

I stuffed the letter from the bank back into the drawer and slipped into the kitchen to turn the vent out toward Pig Park. The smell of cinnamon and butter escaped into the street.

Living above Burciaga's Bakery—and being a Burciaga—meant it was my job to keep the kitchen spotless and to do any other number of things from bringing in the mail to answering the phone.

I was sort of the Cinderella of crumbs—minus the ugly stepsisters and the singing mice.

The last thing we needed was mice.

"How are you doing over there, Masi?" my dad asked.

"All right," I said.

I grabbed a crusty bowl, ran it under hot water and scrubbed hard, scratching at it like it had the kind of itch that requires a good dose of calamine lotion. I tried not to think about the letter.

It wasn't so easy.

See, my dad started the bakery with nothing but an old box of recipes. He liked to say that the bakery, like most of Pig Park, sprouted in the boom and shadow of the American Lard Company. The company had even donated land right in the middle of everything for the park our neighborhood was named after. That's why our neighborhood got named Pig Park, because pig fat made lard and lard had more or less made our neighborhood.

As the company grew, so did we. Hundreds of company employees lived and worked here. They ate and shopped here. We baked twice a day just to keep up. That's until the company closed down, and people left with the jobs.

"Economic downturn." That's how the big wigs at American Lard explained away how our good old Chicago neighborhood got left behind. My dad said that just meant they didn't think they were making enough money. So they packed up their jobs and took them some other place—like a whole other country.

Never mind the irony of American Lard made somewhere other than America.

I knew from that letter in that drawer that with no one to buy the bread, the bakery would close down for good too. We would end up leaving Pig Park like everyone else.

This is what else I knew: I'd lived in Pig Park my whole entire life. I still had a few friends left. So—even after everything—I couldn't wrap my head around the bakery closing and us leaving also. It kept me up at night, wondering about tomorrow and the day after. Maybe I would never see my friends again. My family lived upstairs now. Maybe we'd end up homeless.

My dad was always saying not to think like that, to leave the worrying to him and my mom, but—I just couldn't help it. I couldn't help it about as much as I couldn't help breathing or just being me.

My dad tied an apron around his waist, rolled his sleeves up and grabbed hold of the masa resting on the counter. Sweat dampened his shirt across his thick broad back. He pounded down on dough the color of dirt clay. "How about some music?"

"Music?"

"Yes."

"Like what?" I grabbed a dish towel and dried my hands.

"Anything."

I switched on the radio. My dad sang along to that old song, "Amorcitoooo Corazon." I imagined him making his way down a cobblestone road on a bike—balancing a big basket of freshly baked rolls on his head—belting out the song like in one of those old black and white movies they used to play in the park to bring the neighborhood together.

"Dad, I like it when you sing. It makes me feel like I am all wrapped up in a fuzzy blanket," I said. It made me think of how it was before, when things were good and my dad sang all the time.

My dad sang even louder and smiled like it made him think of it how it was before too.

I felt a little better.

I pulled a sheet of ginger pigs from the oven and put them on the counter to cool. There was no ginger in the pig-shaped treats, just homemade molasses that made the cake-style cookies look like ginger bread when they baked. I grabbed one, broke off a piece, and put it in my mouth. It was perfect—warm, plump and moist on the tip of my tongue.

Sure, I wanted not to worry like my dad said. I'd spent almost every summer of my life in what felt like a 350-degree kitchen. I wanted to spend my summer with my friends outside the bakery for a change. I wanted a chance at being fifteen and "normal." I wanted to make like nothing was wrong.

"Ready?" my dad asked. He untied his apron and threw it down on the counter. I listened for my mom's footsteps on the stairway.

"Yeah." I shoved the rest of the treat into my mouth. Something had to happen.

CHAPTER 2

A family of sparrows scattered into the valley of buildings that loomed large and empty all around Pig Park. I broke away from my parents and walked toward my friend Josefina.

"Hey," I said.

"Good morning, Masi," Josefina said. She undraped the length of her limbs from the bloated slats of the lone park bench that stood among the weeds. I zigzagged through the hodge-podge of folding chairs and plopped down beside her.

There were twenty-five of us: Josefina's family, the families from restaurant row—which was what we called all the surviving eateries on the north side of the park— the Sanchez sisters and their mom, Colonel Franco and Jorge Peregrino. Every girl, boy and grown-up left in our neighborhood sat in a circle. Peregrino made his way toward the center of the group.

I watched with eyes wide open and listened to the

only person in Pig Park still making money. "As you all know, Pig Park has reached out for help and for answers. What is it that draws us to a thing? Most often it's recognition, our senses open up and something in the back of our mind clicks," Peregrino said. He stroked the thick gold chain that hung around the outside of his turtleneck. He pulled out a large piece of paper from his briefcase and waved his hand in front of it like a model on one of those TV game shows. "Behold the solution to Pig Park's problems."

Marcos, Josefina's brother, angled his head. Shiny shoulder length hair swept away from his face and revealed a square jaw line and high cheek bones. He snickered.

Peregrino's visual aid was a map of Pig Park—the actual park our neighborhood was named after—with an oversized cutout of a pyramid from a schoolbook or a magazine taped to it.

Josefina looked at Marcos with thick brown eyebrows in a scrunch. I looked at my dad. My dad looked at my mom. My mom crossed her arms over her chest, shook her head from side to side and sighed.

I squinted at the picture just to make sure. "He wants us to fix Pig Park by putting up a giant pyramid right smack in the middle of everything?" I asked.

"How is this going to help?" my dad asked. He leaned forward on the lopsided legs of his chair, facing Peregrino. My mom reached out and grabbed my dad's chair to keep him from spilling onto the grass.

"You have to think of it like the Picassos downtown. Except no one this side of North America has a pyramid. Building a *Gran Pirámide* right here is the opportunity of a lifetime," Peregrino said.

"What are you talking about?" Mr. Nowak, Josefina's dad, interrupted. Mrs. Nowak squeezed his large white hand with her small brown one.

Peregrino didn't miss a beat. "Pyramids are among the most recognizable symbols in the history of mankind, from Egypt to MesoAmerica. Think of the Aztecs, the Mayans and the Incas. People will see it and come. First out of curiosity, then more. There will be so many people, you won't know what hit you. They will be good people too, the kind who care about history and culture."

"That's your thinking? We're going to keep from becoming a ghost town neighborhood or a massive parking lot by putting up a pyramid for people to gawk at?" Mr. Nowak didn't miss a beat either. "THAT'S going to help my grocery store?"

Josefina turned to me in that way she always had since kindergarten and whispered. "That's crazy."

"Seriously. We're not Aztecs," I said.

"How much is it going to cost?" My mom stood and bellowed over us. It was typical for her to ask about money. The stress of tracking the bakery's accounts was turning her hair to ash and stamping crow's feet into the corners of her eyes.

"You decide how to build it and how much to spend. I didn't come up with this idea on my own. The man who came up with it, Dr. Humberto Vidales Casal, is a world-renowned scholar and community development expert who cures neighborhoods. He knows his stuff. There is a small fee for his guidance. However, when we are finished, *La Gran Pirámide* will more than pay for itself," Peregrino said.

"Well, that doesn't sound so bad," my dad said. He rose to stand beside my mom. "It's an investment." Some of the grown-ups from restaurant row, like Mr. Fernandez and Mrs. Sustaita, nodded. Mr. Nowak clicked his tongue. A few of the others grumbled.

Colonel Franco cleared his throat. "It's better than doing nothing. We don't even need that much money. We have other resources." Despite the Pancho Villa mustache, Colonel Franco wasn't some long lost revolutionary hero. He was a retired Army man and president of the Pig Park Chamber of Commerce. He didn't own a business, but thirty-plus years of bravery, leadership and service to the U.S. of A meant something. He had built bridges in Iraq and Afghanistan as a senior officer. "A pyramid is little more than simple geometry. Two triangles here, two triangles there. I can lead the construction project," he said and waved his hand.

The grown-ups huddled together. Colonel Franco had hit on it with fewer words: a crazy plan had to be better than no plan at all. After a long while, even Mr. Nowak was drawing short breaths around the thing. They were desperate enough that they decided every neighborhood girl and boy would report to the park to help Colonel Franco with the construction. They said it as if it were the most ordinary thing in the world, as if we knew how to do that sort of thing. They less enthusiastically agreed to scrape together what little money we had for Dr. Vidales Casal's fee and wire it to him by the end of the week.

Applause came in small bursts like the kernels in a microwaveable popcorn bag.

Peregrino folded the drawing and stuffed it back into his briefcase.

What else was there to say? I waved goodbye to Josefina and followed my parents home. I took one tiny step after another. My parents shrunk further and further away. I walked as slow as my body would go.

I thought hard about the morning's events. It'd all happened so fast like cars on the expressway, shooting by so quick you wouldn't want to get caught in the way of one. I didn't know exactly what to make of it.

Then something clicked.

My right leg tap-danced with no direction from me. My cheeks pushed up against my ears.

I would get to spend the summer outside with my friends.

CHAPTER 3

The small hand on the clock hovered over the six. I pulled the bakery's blinds and locked the door. I walked upstairs and down the hall.

"We can't do this. We won't even cover our costs this year. We don't have money for that man's fee," my mom said to my dad.

So much for trying to find the positive in this.

My mom pushed her fingers through the ash of her hair. She waved the envelope I recognized as the letter from the bank in the air and lectured my dad about money with all the passion of one of those TV preachers.

"You heard, it'll more than pay for itself," my dad said.

A few things had kept the bakery afloat. My parents owned the building and the equipment—though the equipment was old and worth little more than a cumin seed. There was no payroll since my mom, dad and I were unpaid employees. But we still had to pay utilities, supplies, taxes and permits. My dad had mortgaged the building the year before just to get by.

"We have enough," my dad insisted. "We'll put off some of the bills a little longer."

"Dad, Mom," I interrupted. Both turned to look at me. "Are we going to be okay?"

Neither answered.

"We're working things out," my dad finally said. "You just worry about getting to the park tomorrow." My mom shook her head from side to side and chewed on her bottom lip. She walked away.

Of course, they couldn't just say everything was wonderful or everything was going to crap. They couldn't know for sure. The bakery had seen its share of struggles already.

According to my dad's stories, my abuelita Carmelita Burciaga—his mother—was a widow who'd made ends meet by taking in other people's laundry back in Mexico. She'd accepted a baker as a second husband so that my dad would learn a respectable trade. My dad's then narrow frame, once fragile like the spine of a book, had grown straight and strong from kneading masa and from not toiling in the sun. It had been good going until the torrid summer the baker died. His blood relatives evicted my abuelita and my dad straightaway. They departed with nothing but a suitcase and a box full of recipes.

My dad took a job unloading and loading corn trucks from dawn 'till dusk so he could raise enough money for a bus ticket to come north across the border. While he'd dreamed of California or Texas, he'd ended up here.

He stepped off that bus in the dead of winter—January. The soggy gray city had made dreaming dismal.

The factories were angry monsters, but a means to an end. He took a job at the American Lard Company and roomed with co-workers. The group of men slept in shifts and rows on the floor of a studio apartment. His wages paid for the necessary with any leftovers tucked away. June arrived, and the humid heat was a stark contrast to the desert of his boyhood. He thought there could be no greater evil than the smell of boiling pig fat. Inhaling the fumes from the hot vats of lard slowed him down. But by the end of his fifth year, he started looking at properties and found a place just across the street from the park.

My abuelita Carmelita sold everything she owned to come and help him. Together, they raised enough for a decent down payment. They financed the rest with an uncle's help. As soon as they collected the keys, they moved in. They named the bakery Burciaga's. My dad hand-carved a wooden sign on rosewood, oiled it and hung it outside the door. They bought equipment, leaning on the building's credit line as collateral. They invested every last penny they had and then some.

They sold everything they baked by mid-morning the first day. They even took orders for the next week. Things seemed to be looking up.

A few months later, my dad found my grandmother lying on the kitchen floor, dead of a brain aneurism. His world crumbled. Despite the loss, my dad pushed on.

"Are we going to be okay?" I looked at my dad.

My dad couldn't give a simple answer to my question because he was hopeful. He was willing to gamble, but it wasn't just up to him or my mom or me. Our entire neighborhood was on the line. The Nowaks, the Sanchezes, the Fernandezes, the Sustaitas, the Wongs and everyone else had as much of a stake in this.

I hurried up the stairs. I walked into my room and threw myself down on my bed. One thing was clear. This wasn't MesoAmerica. MasaAmerica maybe. Or even MasiAmerica.

We weren't Egyptians or Aztecs. As a matter of fact,

we weren't exactly one thing. My dad was as Mexican as a mariachi hat, but my mom had grown up right down the street. Josefina was half Polish. The Sanchez sisters had a daddy no one ever talked about. And so on.

Despite these strikes against the new plan, I still wanted to be hopeful like my dad. I would chase hope, wrestle it down and hold on to it like him.

I tried to tuck my worries about tomorrows to the back of my head. I pushed them under a doormat. I locked them in a closet with el cucuy and my other childhood monsters. I put them in my mouth and let them sit there like bites of stale bread until they softened enough for me to swallow.

CHAPTER 4

I scrubbed at the mixing bowls. One of the problems with being stuck inside the bakery all day was that I was sure all the more interesting distractions were somewhere else. I thought myself into a circle—or maybe a knot—like a dog chasing its tail.

I arrived at an impasse. Like I said, even if things didn't work out, at the very least my friends and I would get to spend our last summer together.

It was something like my last meal or —since I was the Cinderella of crumbs—having a fairy godmother grant me one last wish.

I hurried to the park.

I tugged on the belt loops of my dad's old jeans as I jogged. They hung low around my waist and the torn dingy hems dragged on the ground.

"Lovely outfit, Masi," Josefina said. She pointed at my T-shirt. The white jersey was spotted with grease like someone had flung spoonfuls of butter at me.

"Likewise. You make a fine chorizo," I threw back. Josefina had, with all the skill of a sausage maker, squeezed herself into a pair of gym shorts she'd probably outgrown back in eighth grade.

Josefina's thick eyebrows locked into a menace. I mimicked her face. Her scowl deepened. "Not funny," she said, right before her face melted into laughter.

I shrugged. "These are my work clothes. I got no one to impress."

Marcos stepped forward from behind a nearby tree. He reached upward and pulled his hair back behind his ears. "What am I, fried cheese?" he asked.

I put my hands on my hips. "How long have you been here?" I demanded.

Marcos walked to my side in one stride. Josefina turned her shoulder and ignored him as was mandatory of younger sisters. Marcos grinned so that his high cheeks dimpled. "Long enough to hear everything, chorizos." He jabbed his index finger into my arm like I was his little sister too.

I lost my train of thought. If I had to be completely honest—like if someone was pelting me with dried masa balls—I sometimes suffered unsisterly feelings towards him. Maybe it was that he'd grown out his hair. Or maybe I was just a sucker for dimples. I fought the feelings off, of course.

"Ow. Keep your hands to yourself." I rubbed at my arm. I thought back at what Josefina and I had talked about. Relief washed over me. We hadn't said anything particularly embarrassing. "We didn't even say anything. You're so weird," I said.

"Whatever," Marcos said. He strolled back to the tree and pulled his music player out of the front pocket of his Old McDonald overalls. He pulled his headphones on, let his hair fall into his face again, leaned back against the trunk, and closed his eyes.

I made a real effort to ignore him, just like Josefina had, and turned away. Casey and Stacey Sanchez trudged towards us from their mother's flower shop across the street from the north side of the park, wearing cotton candy-colored sundresses—of all things. The boys from restaurant row also arrived in pairs. Frank and Freddy Fernandez wore rancho wear, Pedro Wong sported a tracksuit and little Iker Sustaita sported too-large fatigues—I suspected hand-me-downs from his grandfather. Colonel Franco trailed in at the end.

He moved like a slow shadow at sunset.

He paused next to Josefina and me. I nodded—a tight chin chop. He nodded back. He rubbed at his knee—I suspected an old war injury—just above the hem of his cargo shorts. "Do you want to sit, Colonel?" I asked. "We can move over by the park bench."

"No thank you, Masi. I don't know about you kids, but I'm done sitting around."

He cleared his throat. We all gathered around him. His lips moved and the jet-black broom above his mouth brushed the air in front of his face. "Good morning, everyone. I'm here because I want to be here. I hope you want to be here too."

"Yes," I said.

"Yes, Grampa, sir," Iker said.

"Think of this as summer camp," Colonel Franco said. "What we're doing is important. Everyone has something to contribute. Our first task is to collect bricks and bring them to the park."

I nodded.

"Let's take it from the American Lard Company, tear the place down brick by brick and use it for the pyramid," Marcos said.

"That would be stealing," Colonel Franco said.

The company's four massive buildings sat forgotten at our neighborhood's borders. I doubted anyone would even notice. "But, isn't building on Pig Park stealing too?" I asked. If Colonel Franco was going to be a stickler for the law, I figured we didn't own the park either.

"The park was established by the American Lard Company for its employees. They turned it over to the neighborhood when they left. The Chamber of Commerce administers a land trust."

My mouth dropped open. Colonel Franco may as well have been talking military code. Everyone stared at him, not just me.

"The park belongs to the people who still live here. Technically, we're not doing anything illegal," he explained.

The idea that we owned the park translated to chaos. Marcos pantomimed marking his territory like a dog. The Fernandez brothers cackled in that way that I sometimes heard all the way down the street when they worked the line at their family's tamale shop. The two paced the lawn like a couple of roosters in cowboy boots and staked out their own sections.

Colonel Franco put his fingers to his mustache and whistled loud enough to blow a lung. He raised his left hand and counted down from five using his fingers. Everyone stopped. "Go grab anything you can find with wheels so we can start."

"We don't have driver's licenses," Josefina said.

"Grab anything that doesn't require a driver's license. Meet me in my back yard," he barked.

I elbowed Josefina. "Quit it. He's already annoyed. He'll send us all back home."

"I wish," Josefina said. "He won't send us away. He wants our help."

I didn't want to take that chance. "Let's just do what he says anyway. This isn't so bad," I said.

"It isn't so great." Josefina rolled her eyes. "It's just more work on top of our chores at home."

"At least we get to be out here together."

Her mouth formed a small o as if she hadn't thought of it herself. "I guess you're right," she said.

We borrowed a cart from the Nowak Grocery Store and pushed it to Colonel Franco's backyard. Colonel Franco's entire fence was lined with rows of brick like the back lot of one of those home improvement stores. I looked twice just to take it all in. "I wonder where all this stuff came from."

"I bet he was building a bomb shelter." Josefina stepped closer.

Iker walked up next to us with a wheelbarrow. "It's old Army surplus. Grampa doesn't like to see anyone throw anything away," he said

"Okay," Colonel Franco called from the back stoop where he sat smoking a cigar, knee propped up on a well-worn phonebook. "Now, load the brick and run it over to the park."

"You heard the boss," Pedro Wong said. He appointed himself second-in-command. He wasn't even second-in-command at Wong's Taco Shop, but having grown a paltry mustache over the last year, turning eighteen and being the oldest in our group gave him delusions of authority. He picked up a stack of bricks and started an assembly line of sorts. "Iker and the Sanchez sisters, you guys man the carts. Push the bricks to the park, and bring the carts back. The Fernandez brothers and I will come along and stay at the park to unload. The rest of you stay here and continue loading for the next pick up."

"I don't want to get dirty," Casey, the older and plumper Sanchez sister, said.

"Don't worry. I got this," Iker said. He puffed up his posture to make himself seem bigger and grabbed the wheelbarrow once it was full. He pushed the wheelbarrow away. The Sanchez sisters followed— their two thick silhouettes sashayed close behind him.

Marcos bent down and picked up some bricks. He handed first Josefina and then me a stack. We loaded them onto the grocery store cart. We repeated the process. I lifted heavy trays onto the racks at the bakery. Josefina and Marcos were used to lifting product crates and kitchen stock. Our new task should've been easy, but the sun was relentless. It shone brighter and hotter with each brick. Even an Olympic weightlifter couldn't have muscled away the hot sticky air. I blotted the sweat off my brow with my shoulder. At least I wasn't feeling self-conscious on top of it all. There was too much other discomfort for that, right? We'd all seen each other sweat before anyway.

"You'd think the sun was trying to burst out of the sky," I said.

Josefina huffed. "Ugh, this is terrible," she said.

"We all smell like Marcos' gym socks."

"Like flowers." Marcos grinned and handed me another stack of bricks. "Dumb sun."

"No. I don't mind the sun. I mean, we need the sun, especially if we're going to pass for Aztecs," Josefina said. She held up a sun-ripened arm. Her face contorted into a smile. Marcos and I broke into laughter. Josefina had the complexion of a dinner roll. Even under all the layers of sun, sweat and dirt, she was several shades lighter than Marcos and me.

I smiled at Marcos and Josefina. The sun softened us up like butter on a frying pan. There was more laughter and less complaining as the day wore on.

CHAPTER 5

I squinted at the two large flowers in full bloom moving towards us in the distance. There wasn't a single rumple on the Sanchez sisters' sundresses. It was quitting time, and the sisters had obviously done little work. Casey's surprisingly lithe hand flew in the air and waved a box of paletas. Josefina ignored her and dragged the cart toward the grocery store.

Marcos sprinted across the street towards Casey and Stacey. They cooed and giggled at him. He chatted them up and returned holding a popsicle. "You want some, Masi?" He licked it and pushed it toward me.

"You already put your tongue all over it." I pushed his hand away. He devoured the rest of the popsicle and stuck the stick in the back pocket of his overalls. "That's gross," I added for good measure.

"Roll us home." Josefina nudged the cart in Marcos' direction.

"No, you'll break it," he said. I gave him a dirty

look. Josefina gave him something even dirtier than my look. It involved a finger. Marcos shoved past Josefina. "Come on, Masi. Let's race," he said.

"No." I shook my head, but thought better of it. Marcos had asked, and I had nothing better to do than to go home and stew in my own worry.

Take that other letter in my parents' letter drawer that I didn't want to think about. The school district had sent out a notice at the beginning of summer informing my parents that they were closing down American Academy. We would be bused to the next nearest school in the fall. Most kids might think there was nothing better than having their school close down. On test days, I wished it would.

But I didn't want a new school or new friends. I already had a best friend.

Josefina and I had chosen each other to begin with. On the first day of kindergarten, I'd stuck to my mom's side like a grease stain. "Look, don't you want to make friends?" my mom had asked. Josefina noticed me crying beside my mom and came up to me. She grabbed my hand, and we walked into school together. We'd been as good as sisters ever since. As for Marcos, some days he was really nice. Some days he was unbearable. Josefina said that's exactly what having a brother was like. I'd never told either of them about my sometimes crush. So he treated me no different than his sister. I tried not to think about how much I would miss the Nowaks if we didn't save Pig Park.

"Wait," I said to Marcos.

"Races don't wait, Masi. That's like asking the wind to wait." Marcos tugged on my hair and sprinted past me toward the American Lard Company's immense fenced-in parking lot, which sat barren as a desert on the north side of Pig Park.

"Whatever," I yelled. I took hold of the cart's plastic handlebar, tightened my grip and barreled after him.

My shirt clung to my skin as I ran. The gap between us grew wider and wider. He looked back and mouthed the words "toooooo sloooow." It was as if to say that there was no point in chasing him—and, of course, that was true on more than one level. Marcos became a dot, then nothing. He was halfway to the equator. I gave up and stopped. That's the way it always went with Marcos. I flipped the cart on its side and boosted myself up to grab hold of the windowsill of one of the company's buildings. I peered into the darkness. I yelled my name through a broken pane, "Maaaasi!" Nothing came back, not even an echo.

"I don't know how you can still move," Josefina said over my shoulder.

I turned the cart right side up and pushed south. "I don't know either." I pulled at my sleeves and looked at my arms, but there was nothing to see. Not even a sunburn like Josefina's.

"What does that doctor guy even know? He lives a million miles away from Pig Park," Josefina said. She meant Dr. Vidales Casal, the man who had come up with the idea to build a pyramid in the first place. "I mean, I looked him up. His website says he's president of the Autonomous University of New Mexico, on top of being a professor and a bunch of other stuff."

"What about the president of Mexico?"

"You're not paying attention."

"Let's stop for a second," I said. I stretched out on a nearby patch of grass. I kicked off my shoes and wiggled my stubby brown toes through the cool blades. I pulled a tube of chapstick from my pocket and slathered on the melted strawberry-flavored balm.

Josefina plopped down on the curb. She rubbed her scalp with one hand and her neck with the other. "My hair hurts. I'm done. I'm not coming back tomorrow."

It was a punch to the gut, as if I'd stumbled into a pile of bricks. My chapstick fell in the grass and rolled into the gutter. I let it vanish into the sewer, and just stared at Josefina.

"Don't look at me like that," she said.

"It's hard not to."

"I don't want to come back. My mom pawned all her jewelry—even the stuff my grandma left her when she died— to help pay for this scheme. She used to stare at that stuff and cry herself to sleep. She's probably never getting it back. I don't even care anymore. Look at what happened with Otto," she said. Otto was a boy she'd fallen in love with the year before. His father had found a job downstate just before the summer, and they'd moved away. "It makes me want to leave too. It makes me not care about a lot of things."

I didn't know what to tell her. I didn't know anything about that kind of love. I wanted to—I wished I could meet a boy who saw me as more than his little sister— but that obviously hadn't happened.

But I did know something about a different kind of love. Josefina's words made me feel like I didn't matter. I was a speck of pollen drifting past her. I wanted Josefina to care and to want to fight to stay together. I wanted our friendship to mean something. I didn't say anything. We sat there in silence.

"Hot, hot, HOT!" Josefina blurted. She fanned herself with her hand. "It's time to go."

I stood up. I wasn't ready to let Josefina quit. She

just needed to give it time. "Think about it," I said. Josefina shrugged. I pushed the cart to the grocery store for her, then stomped off in the opposite direction towards the bakery.

CHAPTER 6

A boy I didn't recognize rounded the corner from one of the American Lard Company's vacant buildings. His eyes drank in everything around him.

He was older, but not a grown-up. He wasn't dressed to work like the rest of us. He wore pressed khakis, a plain but tidy blue polo shirt, and carried a backpack. His skin was the color of toast.

Maybe he was lost. Although the company's buildings blocked Pig Park from the expressway and any major roads, the train stopped right here. People still rode those trains from their crummy downtown jobs stapling papers and cleaning buildings to get to the neighborhoods west of us, then back downtown the next day. I'd seen those train cars bursting at the seams like Josefina in her gym shorts. It was possible to get off by mistake.

Or maybe he was one of the people who were supposed to come on account of the pyramid. Never mind that we hadn't even built it yet.

I looked at the train stop, then the boy, then back again. I closed my eyes and opened them. The boy vanished. Maybe the boy had been wishful thinking or a mirage. It was hot enough for it.

I made my way into the bakery. I was downright delirious.

"This is nuts," my mom said to my dad. I tuned them out and climbed the back stairs to my room, two at a time, as fast as I could.

I ignored the shuffle of footsteps behind me.

I sat on the edge of my bed and shook off each shoe without bothering with the shoelaces. Gravity pulled my socks off along with my shoes.

My mom paused in front of my bedroom doorway and took a few steps toward me. "Can I come in?" she asked.

"Sure," I said. I lay back into my bed.

My mom crossed the length of the room and sat on my desk chair. "I see Colonel Franco's been working you kids hard."

"I don't mind. I like helping."

"I know you do. I have something so you don't wake up sore tomorrow," she said. She left the room and returned with a small white can. She pried it open and showed me the kiwi-colored balm. She dipped her fingers into the goop and dabbed the stuff along the outside of my arms in a circular car waxing motion. My skin tingled.

"This isn't going to be easy," she said.

"I don't mind. It's okay so far."

My mom sighed—deep and profound. It dawned on me that maybe she wasn't just talking about the bakery or the pyramid. What was she talking about then? And what was it with everyone? My dad had it right, belting out a song when things got tough. The man was more animated than one of those classic Disney movies these days.

"It's okay," I repeated to my mom. But I wasn't sure it was okay. I lay my head on her shoulder for a minute. I put my hand over my mouth and yawned. "I need to change. I have to finish my chores so I can go to bed and get up early again tomorrow."

"Leave the chores tonight if you're too tired. I'll take care of them."

"Don't do that. I just need a minute." I pulled my pillow over my head until I heard the door close. My body would be fine. I didn't know about the rest of me. I was hallucinating. Josefina was ready to jump ship. Now something was up with my mom.

I tried to think about something—anything—else. I stood up and channeled all my energy into my bakery chores. I washed the dishes, wiped the counters, swept the floor.

When there was no more cleaning left to do, I

went back to my room and barricaded myself in. I drew the blinds in an already dark room. I braided my hair, washed my face, took off my jeans, and lay back down on my bed.

I picked up a magazine, flipped through it, and threw it aside.

I thought back and counted the loads of brick we sent to the park in my head. One, two, three, four, five... We would finish in no time at that rate. I couldn't help myself. My thoughts shifted to the boy from the park. I'd only seen him from afar. He was sort of a blur by now, but I hoped that he was as real as me. The presence of a newcomer would mean things were actually turning around. And, honestly, with everything else, it felt nice to think of him.

My eyelids dropped like ten-pound sacks of flour.

CHAPTER 7

The heat of the sun seeped between the slats of the blinds, warming my face. I rubbed the sleep out of my eyes. The sun was high enough to leak through my window, which meant I was late—very late.

I threw on my jeans and ran across the street.

Our group huddled in the center of the park. I pushed my way in. Casey Sanchez stood at the center. She wore a cut up styrofoam bowl tied around her neck with a belt. The homemade neck brace pushed the meat of her cheeks up like two bulging slabs of menudo. "What happened?" I asked. "Did you fall down the stairs at home or something?"

Casey grimaced and moaned.

Colonel Franco shook his head from side to side. "She got hurt yesterday. The boys will finish what we were doing with the bricks. You girls come with me to the Chamber of Commerce office," he said.

Josefina was a red-faced beast ready to strike.

"I'm pulling you out of the field. It's not safe," Colonel Franco continued.

I couldn't tell if he was serious. It didn't seem like Casey had lifted a finger the day before. Besides, if it came down to a safety issue, everyone needed to go. Not just the girls.

"But—" I started and stopped. I shut my mouth. Banishment to the Chamber office was still a step up from being sent home.

I followed Josefina to the Pig Park Chamber of Commerce office, which was located in Colonel Franco's basement. Stacey grabbed hold of the wheelbarrow, and Casey squeezed her body inside it. The wheelbarrow's wheels squealed in protest. Stacey pushed hard and kept up the pace. She panted, but held her head up high like she was doing something very important.

"They're like two great big toads on parade," Josefina snarled under her breath.

I smothered a smile with my hand. Casey did look like a great big toad. At least they were wearing regular jeans and T-shirts this time.

Colonel Franco's basement was dark and humid. A fluorescent bulb and two small windows didn't brighten the room. The small oscillating fan blew air with all the power of a pinwheel.

It was just how a person might imagine. There were medals—commendations for service in several wars—all along one wall.

Colonel Franco ripped a dartboard from the opposite wall and took a case of beer out of the refrigerator—I assume to keep it out of reach. He carried everything away and returned with a large whiteboard. He hung it on the wall in place of the dartboard.

Casey and Stacey collapsed on the sagging couch in the corner. Josefina and I sat on the leftover stools around a card table.

"We need permits to build. You will help me fill out the paperwork. You'll fill out applications to file," Colonel Franco said. I swallowed and heard the saliva making its way down my throat. It was that quiet. I looked to Josefina. Her face was a perfect emoticon of anger. Her lips pursed tight until they curved downward into a downward parenthesis.

"We don't even know how we're building it yet," I said.

"I suppose that would be a problem. I'm about done drawing up the plans. You can write letters to government officials so they know that we're real people asking for real things, meanwhile. This is just as important as lugging bricks. I won't ask you to like it, but that's what you'll do," Colonel Franco said. He cracked his neck.

He moved to his desk. He pushed the big button on his computer. The fat screen hummed and vibrated, struggling to reanimate. Several minutes passed. He pulled out a box of pencils, paper, and a list of names and addresses and slid them across the table in front of us. "There is only one computer anyway."

"Can we at least get a radio or a TV?" I asked. We needed something to cut the tension.

"Please." Josefina finally opened her mouth.

"Please. Please," Casey and Stacey joined in.

"We'll see," he grumbled. He disappeared. He reappeared after a minute with one of those antique televisions sets with rabbit ear antennas. I could see what Iker meant about his grandpa never throwing anything away. He put the TV down and disappeared again.

I flipped through a series of fuzzy channels and settled on the black and white movie station.

A movie called *The Devil and Daniel Webster* came on. I'd seen it before. A man cuts a deal with the devil in order to get rich. He becomes filthy rich at his town's expense. Little by little, he loses control. The devil comes to collect. Daniel Webster, the hero, sues the devil for the man's soul on the basis of his American citizenship.

"Would any of you ever sell your souls?" I asked.

"Sure, to be rich." Stacey answered. "Besides I got a God-given American right to sell anything I want."

"You don't have any rights. Look at yourself. Not with a name like Sanchez," Casey said.

"This isn't Arizona—or Alabama," Stacey shot back. I had opened a can of Sanchez. They bickered like two old ladies over coffee. I was sorry I'd asked.

"We better do some work if we ever want to get out of here," I interrupted. I'm not sure why Casey and Stacey listened to me, but neither muttered another word. The pair leaned over their stacks of papers and scribbled.

"Wish it had been that easy an hour ago," Josefina said.

I shrugged. My toes danced against the linoleum below. I stared at the paper in front of me. My fingers were warm and moist around the pencil. I looked over at Josefina's letter. She'd written a standard Please help us / Thank you letter. I wondered how many Please help us / Thank you letters anyone should ever have to read. I tapped the tip of the eraser against my forehead until the words rattled out, and I began writing.

My name is Masi Burciaga. I am fifteen years old, and I have lived in Pig Park my whole life. My family owns a bakery here. We are among the few who didn't move away when the American Lard Company closed down. That may change soon if we don't find a way to bring people back.

So a bunch of us want to hang out, build a pyramid in the middle of Pig Park and save our neighborhood. Are you in?

I was rambling, but I didn't care. I copied the text onto a clean sheet. I copied it again and again, changing the 'dear whomever' part each time. My knuckles turned white and a soft bump began to form on my middle finger.

When Colonel Franco came in and announced that we could go home, I jumped up and placed my stack of letters on his desk. I rushed upstairs and breathed in the thick hot air.

Josefina stood outside. She patted her face and winced. "I told you. It's time to throw in the towel. This feels more like summer school than summer camp. These letters aren't going to do anything. Who even reads letters written in pencil anymore? This isn't nineteen ninety-two."

"At least your skin will have time to heal," I said. Once again, I didn't know what else to say to her. I could see her point. She was right about the letters. I was sure they would end up under a pile of coffee-stained papers that everyone would forget.

I hadn't escaped the bakery for this. If that boy from the park was real and came back, I would miss it. It was a silly thing to suddenly think about, so I didn't say anything to Josefina. As much as I couldn't bear to sit in Colonel Franco's basement one more day, I also didn't want Josefina to have another reason to throw in the towel. At least we were still together.

We walked to the south end of the park where we found the boys clearing the overgrown grass from an area marked off by blue duct tape, about eighty by eighty feet, a perfect square. It looked to be about one eighth of the park. They were also digging a trench along the tape.

Marcos looked up and jogged over to us. I caught myself eyeballing his biceps—the way they strained against the cotton of his shirt as he ran. What was it with me? Maybe the summer heat was making me boy crazy. I told myself not to stare.

"Did you miss me today, Masi?" His hand shot up and tucked his hair behind his ear.

"About as much as I missed scrubbing dishes," I said, a little too quick.

"I think that's a yes."

Red inched up my cheeks. I changed the subject. "What are you doing tomorrow?"

"We're digging out the rest of the trench along each side of the pyramid," he said. Marcos grinned and ran back to where the other boys were still working.

"Your brother is weird."

"Ugh. I can't believe we're related sometimes." Josefina crossed her arms over her chest and paced back and forth. "Masi, I don't want to shovel dirt any more than I want to write letters, but it would serve Casey and Stacey right if we figured out a way to get Colonel Franco to let us work outside again. They're not going to be the reason everything changes for me. I get to decide."

A smile crept onto my face. I didn't care about Casey and Stacey. It only mattered that it made Josefina want to stick around for the time being. Everything would go back to normal once we saved Pig Park.

CHAPTER 8

My fingers tightened around the extra cookie cutter. I was tired of sweeping up crumbs and doing things that didn't seem to matter, like writing. I waved the aluminum pig outline high in the air. "Can I help you, Dad? I already scrubbed the dishes?" I begged.

"Are your hands clean?" he asked.

I pushed my free hand up to his face. "My hands are just about clean. We're only writing letters." I couldn't help complaining.

"Letters?"

"Yeah, boring stuff."

"I'm sure Colonel Franco has his reasons."

I looked at my dad for a second. I wanted to tell him all about Casey and the homemade neck brace, but I decided not to. I didn't want to put the idea of me getting hurt in his head. It would just worry him. Then he wouldn't want us at the park either.

"Don't just stand there. Wash your hands." My dad

waved his rolling pin in a shoo away motion. "La, de, da…"

I moved to the sink.

The bell we put out when we left the front room unattended rang. My dad hurried out. I pushed the door a crack to see. Colonel Franco stood a few feet from my dad.

"Good afternoon, Tomás." He nudged someone toward my dad. "This is a student of Dr. Vidales Casal. He'll be staying with Jorge Peregrino at his warehouse for the summer." I pinched myself. The boy from the park stood in the middle of the room wearing a red polo shirt this time.

"Nice to meet you, sir. I'm Felix Diaz." Felix said. He grabbed my dad's hand between his two hands and shook it. His voice was soft, not like Colonel Franco's grating consonants and vowels.

"Dr. Vidales Casal's university in New Mexico will give Felix school credit for volunteering. A couple of kids will be coming up from the school," Colonel Franco continued.

"Masi, come here." My dad pulled the door open. I was leaning against it. I lost my balance and stumbled into the room. "This is my daughter, Masi."

I nodded at Colonel Franco, then wiped my moist palm on the leg of my pants. I pushed it toward Felix. My nose aligned with the tiny embroidered lizard on his shirt. I looked up. He was very good looking up close. He had cat eyes—pupils so large it was hard to tell what color his irises were. He blinked. Two curtains of lashes floated against his cheeks.

Felix squeezed my hand. He sauntered across the room, looking through the glass cases at the bread on the trays. The labels on the shelves read: *conchas, cuernitos, bolillos, marranitos*—aka conch-shaped sugar-topped loaves, croissants, white baguette style rolls, and ginger pigs.

"Have a taste, Felix," my dad said.

Felix picked up a large fluffy conch. He tore off pieces and stuffed them in his mouth until it was nothing but sugar dust on his shirt. "Delicious. I wish I could make this myself."

"You bake?" my dad asked with a grin.

Felix laughed. "I try every now and then. Nothing this good." Felix went on about how he could make out the taste of lemon rind. He listed out other spices I was surprised he'd even heard of, like anise and cloves. "I decided to minor in chemistry when I discovered an ability to decipher the ingredients in almost anything, but my major is business."

"Very nice. Speaking of business, will you kids excuse us for a minute?" My dad ushered Colonel

Franco toward the door. "What's all this business about these kids writing letters?"

"We're reaching out to some of our public officials," Colonel Franco said.

"Can't Jorge Peregrino just make some phone calls? I know he knows some people in the Mayor's office." My dad was right. Peregrino was more than connected, and he was more than doing okay moneywise. He the richest man in Pig Park. He had made a fortune importing and distributing herbal supplements from south of the border. His customers and friends were everywhere. Big cities, small ones. Rich neighborhoods, poor ones.

Felix walked towards me. "You have an interesting name," he said.

"My mom wanted to name me Tomasina after my dad. My dad didn't like it, so they named me Masi for short. Spelled M-A-S-I, but pronounced Mah-see." His lips parted. He smiled a bleached-tooth smile. Heat rose up my spine. I was suddenly nervous—or some other thing.

"So it's a family name."

"Yep. After my dad."

"How long have you been in business?"

"Since before I was born. Well, my parents have been. I mean." My voice cracked. It was city asphalt in the spring.

I excused myself and ran back to the kitchen. The kitchen door swung closed. I pressed my back against the nearby wall. The voices in the front room carried on a few more minutes.

I waited until I was sure that they were gone and walked back into the room.

My dad smiled like his face was about to split in two. He washed his hands and wrapped up the ball of masa sitting on the counter. "This thing seems to be catching speed," he said.

"Yes." I wiped down his work area.

My mom entered the room and headed for the register. I glanced at the clock. It was ten minutes past seven: closing time. "We had company?" she asked.

"Colonel Franco was here." My dad drew the blinds. He turned the deadbolt on the door. "Dr. Vidales Casal sent a boy to help. Colonel Franco came to introduce him. He seemed nice."

"You didn't call me. I would like to have met him."

"You were taking a nap," my dad said.

"I was tired." My mom pulled out the register's tray with such force that a coin flew out. There were ten singles, two fives, four quarters and a roll of dimes in there—no more than we kept to make change.

I don't know if it was from just waking up, but I

could tell she was in a mood. I backed away and tiptoed upstairs.

I lay in my bed staring at my bedroom ceiling. I thought about Felix's eyes, his lips and his skin the color of toast.

CHAPTER 9

"That's my pencil," Casey said.

"No it's not," Stacey said.

"I bought it!"

"No you didn't!"

They talked non-stop, back and forth, their words flying everywhere, crowding the already small basement. I leaned into Josefina. "Did Colonel Franco visit you guys yesterday?" I asked.

"Sure did," she said. "Colonel Franco walked HIM up and down the street and introduced him to my parents. Do you think the rest of them are that cute?"

"The rest of who?"

"He said more students would be coming to help us."

"I don't know."

"Are New Mexicans supposed to be cute?"

"Same as old Mexicans."

"Very funny."

"I know."

"Old Mexicans like the Colonel?" Casey interrupted.

"Ew. This is a conversation between two, not three," Josefina said. She made a big to-do about turning her chair around so that she was facing me and giving her back to the Sanchez sisters. "That boy sure is something to look at. Even more reason to get outside."

I nodded, relieved at Josefina's changing attitude. Her good mood was contagious. I smiled. Stacey smiled. The Colonel burst into the room. Even he smiled.

He stood in front of us and held up a large paper for us to see. "Okay, girls. I've finished the blueprints. Now, someone dial Jorge Peregrino's number for me."

Josefina grabbed the phone, punched in the number and handed it to him. Colonel Franco didn't waste time with small talk. "Jorge, can you call some of those construction friends of yours? Yes. Tell them that we still want to use the salvaged materials the kids hauled." Colonel Franco nodded, uttered a few *mmms*, and hung up.

The phone rang a couple minutes later. Colonel Franco reached for the phone and pressed it against his ear. "Done," he said. He put down the receiver and sat at his desk. He smiled. "A construction company has just offered to donate and build the support beams for *La Gran Pirámide's* structure."

It all looked so easy. Maybe it was because Peregrino was important or because our pyramid was so extraordinary, but people just wanted to be a part of it like Peregrino had promised. It didn't matter much as long as it got done.

I chewed on my bottom lip and whispered to Josefina. "This could mean we might get back outside sooner than we thought. Let's work on changing Colonel Franco's mind while he's in a good mood."

"I don't want to have to go back outside," Casey said. She pointed to her thick neck. The brace was off, but she wasn't forgetting.

"Shush it. She wasn't talking to you. She was talking to me," Josefina said. "Besides, you barely even got your hands dirty."

"Yeah," I said.

Colonel Franco grabbed his clipboard from the top of his desk. He rapped the wall with it. "Let's not argue, girls. Let's focus on moving forward here. Work on your letters. I'll be back in a bit."

Colonel Franco returned after a few hours and announced that we were done for the day. I stood up and stretched. "I unloaded ten bags of flour this morning, and I feel great," I said as loud as I could.

"Man, my muscles are bigger than Marcos' now. I'm

stronger than any of these boys," Josefina played along. Obviously. I'd seen her brother lately.

Colonel Franco didn't even look our way. He kept his eyes on the stack of papers on his desk. We were going to have to try harder.

"We need to come up with a better plan," I said to Josefina as we walked home.

"You're right," she said. "We'll think of something. We'll get it right. He can't ignore us forever. Don't worry."

CHAPTER 10

Josefina stumbled into me. "Watch it," I said. We stood at the south edge of the park and stared. Colonel Franco and four men in matching Johnson Construction company T-shirts gathered around a crane and a flatbed truck.

Peregrino's donors hadn't wasted any time.

"You girls stand back," Colonel Franco yelled at us. He made a sweeping motion with his hands.

"We just can't catch a break," Josefina said.

"He didn't say to go back to the basement," I said. Josefina smiled. "Do you think that boy will show up here?"

"Anything is possible," she said.

We walked a few feet back. We stopped just short of the sidewalk and gawked. Colonel Franco pulled a roll of paper from his cargo pants. He flattened it against the door of the truck. He pointed to the paper and gestured toward the taped-up area. The workers watched and listened. They blotted sweat beads off their bearded faces with their T-shirts though it wasn't even nine in the morning yet.

One of them grabbed hold of the crane's side view mirror and pulled himself into the driver's seat. He pulled a red handkerchief from his pocket and tied it around his head. "My mom wears one of those to cover her hair when she dusts and sometimes when she mops. Hers is pink." Josefina giggled.

Casey and Stacey Sanchez crossed the street in our direction. "What's all this?" Casey asked. She pulled the ends of the straps of her backpack between her fingers, adjusting the fit and shifting the weight. "What's with all the lumberjacks?"

"They're construction workers, genius." Josefina rolled her eyes. "Can't you see they're carrying metal beams, not axes?"

"They're building the frame," I said.

"When did they get here?" Casey asked.

"They must have pulled up early while we all were sleeping."

"I didn't hear anything," she said.

"Maybe you're too far from the park." I hadn't heard them either, and I lived right across the street. I'd slept through the parade of trucks.

"How did they even get their trucks in?" Stacey asked.

"Good question." Our streets were narrow and difficult for any outsider to navigate. It was a constant source of complaints before the American Lard Company closed down. "How DID they get in?" I echoed Stacey.

"Very carefully," Marcos answered. I turned around. The boys—Marcos, Pedro Wong, Iker and Frank and Freddy Fernandez—had all infiltrated our gawkers' circle.

"Funny," I said. "Aren't you supposed to help them?"

"No one told us," he said.

Pedro Wong cleared his throat. "Let me talk to Colonel Franco for a minute." He walked toward the men. He pointed at us and said something that we were too far away to hear. Colonel Franco shook his head. Both of them walked back in our direction.

"You kids go home for now," Colonel Franco said. I put my hand on my hips. No one in the group moved an inch.

"We want to stay," Marcos said.

Colonel Franco rubbed at his knee. He looked at us. He looked at the men. "Fine. Stay, but keep out of the way. I don't want anyone getting hurt, and I don't want any complaints." He walked back to the truck.

The crane's arm swung down and one of the men grabbed hold of the giant hook dangling from a cable.

I smiled at Marcos. I plopped down on the grass. Marcos sat beside me. Casey pushed up next to Marcos on the other side. She sat down. Her long shorts inched up, exposing her chubby knees. She removed her backpack, laid it on the grass and opened it. It was a treasure chest of junk food. She pulled out a couple of two liter bottles of sodas and several large bags of potato chips. "Want some?" she asked Marcos. His eyes opened wide.

"Careful, she's gonna give you cooties," I said.

"Jealousy doesn't suit you, Masi," he said.

"Ugh. You wish." I shook my head. Maybe Marcos was right. Maybe I felt a little pang of something. But I shook it off. I just wanted to enjoy the feeling that something was happening and that I was outside. I moved over by Josefina and sat down. I imagined we were at one of those long ago movie nights in the park.

Marcos took a bottle of root beer from Casey and chugged. He grabbed a bag of chips and passed it around to everyone. I stuck my hand in and grabbed a fist full of the lime chips. They were tangy, salty and not the kind of breakfast food my mom would approve of.

We sat there and watched the men tie the metal hook around one of the beams. The crane lifted the beam into place inside the trench along the taped off area—then another and so on. They poured concrete into the trench. They manipulated the steel, tilting it inward, at which point the slanting vertical beams met in the center at about sixty feet in the air. Four additional beams were lifted and bolted horizontally to these, ten feet off the air. They repeated this process at twenty feet, thirty feet, and so on.

The whole thing went up like they were playing with Legos. The men walked up and down the length of the beams, testing for stability.

I was glad Peregrino had pulled some strings and gotten us some professional help. There was no way we could've pulled off that kind of job on our own. Despite Colonel Franco's experience, none of the rest of us knew what we were doing.

"Pretty fantastic," I said. I lay back and stared at the lone white cloud in the sky.

It was something like how I'd imagined my summer with my friends. Lying in the grass, toasting in the sun like a tray full of ginger pigs sitting in the oven. I wanted to lay in the grass forever.

CHAPTER 11

The following morning the construction workers packed up their tools, their crane and their other equipment. They jumped in their truck. Colonel Franco walked across the park and into the middle of the street. His hands flew high in the air like a symphony conductor's, and he directed them out.

There was honking, a little bit of cursing, and all around more noise than when they'd arrived. They squeezed out in reverse. Iker stood at the edge of the street waving them off.

I looked past Iker at the brand new beacon of steel at the end of the park and smiled.

Colonel Franco rubbed at his knee and walked in our direction. "You girls go back to the basement. You boys stay here with me," he said.

I dragged my feet down into the dungeon. The Sanchez sisters plopped down on the couch. They shared a magazine and took naps. They scrambled to look busy when Colonel Franco walked in to check for mail and make a phone call on his old land line. "Cell phones give you brain cancer," he said. And, of course, the company's compound of abandoned buildings pretty much blocked off any signal. Most of Pig Park had given up on cell phones long ago. It was a dumb thing to spend money on.

Hours went by.

Then days.

Lying in the grass eroded into a distant memory. The frame of the pyramid hovered above the trees, casting a tall shadow. It was an ever-present reminder of that one great day outside.

Colonel Franco placed a box of envelopes on the table in front of us. "Seal, address and stamp these," he said and walked out.

I grabbed a stack of envelopes and fanned myself with them. I flipped through them, looking at names I didn't recognize. My foot tap-danced against the linoleum under the table.

"Who's paying for all these stamps?" I asked. It was the kind of thing my mother might burst out with. I jumped out of my seat and paced the short length of the basement. "Can't we just send emails? These might as well be smoke signals."

"Relax," Josefina said. "I'm going to take those envelopes and smack you if you don't quit fidgeting."

"I've had it with this. We could be outside. We could be doing so much more."

"Stop whining, you're starting to sound like the rest of us. We just have to keep trying like we did before."

"You're right. I don't know what came over me."

"I think it's called cabin fever." She grabbed a scrap of paper, scribbled on it, and slid it over to me. It read: Meet me at the construction site tomorrow at sunset. Bring some cookies.

Tomorrow is the 4th of July, I wrote back. I looked at the clock. "Time to go." I grabbed my water bottle. I took the paper scrap, tore it into a hundred pieces, and tossed it in the trash can.

Josefina followed me outside. We walked toward the park. Marcos ran toward us. The bricks we'd hauled that first day now lay in color-coded piles beside the steel frame.

"Are you done for the day?" I asked.

"Almost." Marcos panted. "We're sorting bricks so we can start setting them around the frame tomorrow."

"How are you going to get them to slant along the frame without toppling."

"Same way the ancients did, layering, physics, military secrets."

"We're in the middle of something, Marcos. Shoo now," Josefina said.

"So were we." He winked at me, then stuck out his tongue at Josefina. He ran back to the park.

The sun burned high in the sky. "Doesn't he get hot in that?" I pointed at the long sleeved shirt that barred me from looking at Marcos' well-formed biceps.

"Whatever. Don't change the subject. Tomorrow. There." She pointed past Marcos, at the pyramid in progress.

"Seriously?"

"Yes. No one will be around tomorrow. It'll be the perfect time."

"The perfect time for what?"

"The perfect time to get our minds off everything. Just trust me."

I sighed and walked home.

Leave it to Josefina. Colonel Franco didn't care what we said. We needed to find his weak spot. Distractions weren't going to cut it anymore.

CHAPTER 12

Josefina stretched her arms from side to side, and then reached up into the dusk. "Help me," she said.

"Help you what? Do jumping jacks?"

"Get a closer look." Josefina grabbed hold of a steel beam with one hand and my shoulder with the other. She propelled herself up. Once on the beam, she braced herself from her sitting position and helped pull me up. She climbed up the slanted side beams. I struggled behind her until we were just below the tip of the pyramid. We slid onto the top horizontal beam. We faced east, above the treetops, with our legs dangling over the side. We were high enough above the trees to make it hard for anyone to see us.

There were a million lights.

"Wow," I said.

"I told you. Look at all those buildings—and lights."

It was indeed something to behold. We could see everything. Sleek high-rise buildings hovered like monsters just a couple of miles away in downtown. Nice new mid-rise condominiums lined up along the neighborhood east of us. We were the sore at their side. Abandoned buildings jutted out like weeds throughout various other sections of the city. I wondered if each of those had once had their own American Lard Company.

It made me sad for more than my friends. I was sad for Pig Park. I missed the old Pig Park. It dawned on me that I'd never given myself time to be sad about that before. "Thank you for bringing me here," I said.

"No problem. It's the perfect place to watch the city fireworks," she said. "Did you remember to bring it?"

"Yes," I said. I handed Josefina a small plastic bag full of red, white and blue sugar cookies my dad had made special.

"I brought something too." She pulled two cartons of milk from her purse and set them on the beam.

I grabbed one and shook it. I opened my own small bag and put half a cookie in my mouth. I washed it down with the milk.

"It's like we're at the top of the Eiffel Tower," Josefina said. I imagined the Eiffel Tower right smack in the middle of Pig Park instead of the pyramid. The corners of my mouth slowly pushed against my cheeks.

"The Eiffel Tower," I repeated. Was that more or

less ridiculous than a pyramid? Milk made its way out my nose. Laughter came like a painful infection, and Josefina wasn't immune either. I bordered on a medical emergency. I was laughing so hard that I had to wrap my arms around the beams to keep from falling off.

"I don't even know why we're laughing," Josefina said.

"You have some funny ideas!"

She pointed to the buildings downtown. "That's where I'm moving. Marcos and my parents can fend for themselves."

Josefina's comment killed the laughter. I didn't understand. Just the day before, she'd said we needed to keep trying. We were going to save Pig Park and our friendship.

"You can't talk like that," I said.

"Sure I can."

"No. Quit it."

I looked at my hands. I looked at the steel that would be a pyramid. I stuck my fingers through the beam's stud holes, but I couldn't look at her. Josefina didn't say anything.

"I'm coming up," a familiar voice bellowed from below.

Marcos climbed to the top beam. He squeezed in between us. I was never so grateful to see him. He pulled out a paper bag with some kind of bottle from his backpack. He twisted the cap off and held the bottle with the bag still wrapped around it out in the air in front of us.

"I don't even want to know what's in that," Josefina said. "Who invited you anyway?"

Marcos ignored Josefina. "Happy Birthday, America." He took a swig.

"Happy Birthday, America," I repeated after him.

"You want some?" he asked. He pushed the bottle in my direction.

"What is it?"

"Does it matter? Sometimes you just got to live a little, Masi." He took another swig.

Josefina rolled her eyes. I pushed the rest of my cookies at him, having lost my appetite. He devoured them in two bites. Marcos pulled a bag of bbq chips from his backpack.

"Casey must be rubbing off," I said. I looked past him at Josefina.

A manmade fireball flew high and burst in the sky, followed by silence. Josefina was like that fireball—ready to shoot into the sky. The silence was unbearable. "I wonder if the people in those buildings up there get scared when those things come so close," I said.

Five more fireballs ripped into the sky like gunshots.

Josefina's face softened. "No, I bet those sound like bells and look like flower-blossoms up there. I bet you never worry about a single thing when you live in those fancy buildings," she said. Then...I almost understood her. I sometimes found myself wishing I didn't have to worry about a thing either. But it wasn't so easy for me.

"I don't know if it's the 'juice,' but I find it hard to worry about a thing up here too." Marcos tilted back the bottle and guzzled.

I grabbed the bottle from Marcos. If it was all going to crap anyway, then maybe I needed to find a way of making it easier too. I took a giant swig and watched from the corner of my eye as Josefina's jaw nearly separated from her face. It was tart. I brought it to my nose and sniffed it. I handed it back. "It really is just juice," I said.

Marcos laughed.

Josefina raised an index finger to her lips and shushed us. "Did you hear that?" she asked. Marcos and I shook our heads side to side.

"We were careful," I whispered.

"You weren't exactly invisible when I found you," Marcos whispered back. "And we haven't been particularly quiet."

Clink, clink, clink.

There it was. Someone was tapping one of the beams with a coin—or maybe a fingernail.

We edged closer to the beams, then sat as still as possible. I hoped it wasn't Colonel Franco or either set of parents. My heart went bum, bum. BUM, BUM, BUM like a madman with a drum.

CHAPTER 13

I held on tight. I sat as still as the beam. I looked downward without moving my head. My eyeballs inched from one end of my face to the other. It was impossible to see anything.

The figure below turned his face upward. A low flying manmade fireball illuminated the sky behind him.

It was Felix. He waved. We were not invisible.

I'd been more or less holding my breath. I exhaled. I inhaled. My lungs filled. It was as if I'd been running.

"What do you think he's doing here?" Josefina asked.

"I don't know."

"I'll ask him." Marcos volunteered.

"We'll all go talk to him." Josefina undraped her legs from the beam and started down.

Marcos went next. I went last. Going down wasn't any easier than going up. The beams below seemed to shift under my sneakers. I slipped on the last beam. Felix and Marcos both reached out to steady me.

"We were just conducting quality control. Checking the thing out to make sure it's sound," Josefina said to Felix. She rapped on the metal with her knuckles.

"You better not tell anyone, man," Marcos said. Josefina elbowed him. He coughed a little. She gave him the kind of look that would silence a pack of barking dogs.

"From where I'm standing, there's nothing to tell," Felix said.

"We were supposed to be home by nine-thirty." Josefina tapped on her watch.

"Me too," I mumbled.

"I'll walk with you," Felix said.

"Let's all walk together," Marcos said.

"We're going in the opposite direction, Marcos," Josefina said. She dragged Marcos away by the elbow.

Felix stuck his hands in his pocket. I speed-walked in the direction of the bakery. Felix followed close at my side.

"You're probably wondering what I was doing out here," he said. He looked at me with his cat eyes, and I felt that strange thing again. It was like a pair of wings stretched inside my ribcage and fluttered. I pursed my lips tight—hoping to keep my insides from flying out. When I did open my mouth, nothing came out—not my insides and not a word. I couldn't think of anything to say.

"I wanted to get a better look at the fireworks, so I

walked over. Then I heard voices, so I came to check. You guys found the best view of all," Felix continued for me.

"Hmm, we thought we were being quiet."

"You were. Relatively. I just happened to be listening closely."

"You were bored."

"Not at all. Jorge Peregrino has been keeping me busy working on some things. But it's not like much happens where I'm from. There's nothing there but chile pepper fields as far as the eye can see. I have to drive an hour or more just to go to a movie theater. I'm not complaining. I love home, but it just is."

"Pig Park used to have its own fireworks." In the good old days, the American Lard Company had splurged for a small fireworks display in the parking lot.

"Things will turn around."

"They will," I said. I wanted to believe it as much as ever. I looked out into the valley of empty buildings. I refused to buy into Josefina's earlier proclamation about just leaving. I stopped in front of the bakery. "This is me."

"I know that. I've been here, remember?"

"It's late. I should go in. Goodnight."

"Goodnight, Masi."

I don't know why I looked at his mouth, but when I did the world around us stopped.

He had…
masa lips,
textured with fingerprints,
soft as if molded,
soft like warm rolls,
probably soft to kiss…

The heat rose to my face for what I was thinking. The truth was that if fifth-grade dares didn't count, then I'd never kissed anyone before. Josefina had dared Marcos to kiss me—or eat ten giant jalapeños. Marcos hated jalapeños. The kiss had been quick, and I hadn't even closed my eyes.

But this wasn't about Marcos for a change.

I wanted to be invisible more than ever. I hurried inside and locked the door. I ran to my room where I was free to think about anything I wanted to. I lay down on my bed and closed my eyes. I thought about Felix and his soft, soft lips.

CHAPTER 14

"Harrumph," Felix cleared his throat and stepped through the front door. He pushed a pair of thick black plastic reading glasses onto his face.

He tucked a notebook under one arm and a red mechanical pencil behind his ear. He extended his free hand out to my dad in the way people were supposed to at job interviews.

"Masi." Felix nodded at me. I nodded back.

"Masi," my dad said. I nodded again. "Masi," my dad repeated.

"Yes, Dad."

"Go get Felix a chair."

I pulled out a folding chair from the utility closet, and Felix sat down. "Sir," he said.

"What can we do for you this morning, Felix?" my dad asked.

"I'm walking door to door to see how I can help each family prepare for the visitors Dr. Vidales Casal promised."

"Where should we start?"

"We can start with a few questions. I'm sort of figuring it out as we go."

"Okay. Shoot."

"Is your family already doing anything in particular to prepare?"

My dad frowned and his jaw clenched. "Just trying to get by so we can stay open long enough to see it happen."

Felix laughed. "Well, that is certainly important."

My dad's facial muscles relaxed. "Ok. Wait, before we continue. Please have some bread."

I handed Felix a paper plate with a conch on it. The way he devoured the last one, I assumed it was the way to go. Felix tore off large pieces and stuffed them into his mouth. "Okay. First question: how do you make the bread, sir?" he asked with his mouth full.

"Depends which kind."

"How long does it take to make the bread?"

"That also depends."

"How much does it cost to make it?"

"Too much."

"How much money do you guys make on a daily basis?"

"Not enough."

Felix had more questions than the PSAT. Except

some of the questions seemed to cross the line into the personal. My dad didn't act put off. He smiled through the bombardment.

"Can I see the bakery's kitchen, sir?" Felix asked.

"Sure. Come on back and have a look." We followed him into the kitchen. My dad showed Felix the pantry, our kitchenware, and the clunker of an oven. He pulled a sack of flour onto the counter. He opened the refrigerator and took out eggs, milk, and butter. Before long, Felix and my dad were up to their elbows in flour. My dad made talking to Felix look easy.

"How old are you, Felix?" my dad asked.

"Just turned seventeen, sir. I'll be a sophomore in college next fall."

"You are a very smart boy, so young and already your second year in college."

"I skipped fourth and fifth grade. Studying in Dr. Vidales Casal's program will help me finish even earlier. It's an incredible opportunity in many ways. Dr. Vidales Casal built the Zochimilco of Minnesota and the Antigua of California. His ideas have traveled the world: the former Soviet Union, Cuba, Venezuela, Germany, Italy, China and more."

"He sounds like an adventurous man."

"Yes. I'd like to travel someday too. But this is my very first time across state lines."

"Were your parents okay with you coming here by yourself?"

"It's just me and my mom."

He reached out and patted Felix on the shoulder, leaving a flour print on his shirt. "You and I are not so different, Felix. Growing up, it was just me and Mother too. I left her so I could do something better." The way he said it made me feel sorry.

It was all elbows in the kitchen. I squeezed past my dad and made my way back into the front room. I plopped down at the counter next to my mom. She was tracking the bakery accounts on the family laptop. I didn't need to watch to know how bad it was. We were lucky to have what we had. I was lucky to have two parents, no matter the rest. It made me feel even sorrier.

"I'm tired," my mom said after a long while. She went upstairs. I stayed behind and waited for the kitchen to clear out so I could finish my chores.

Felix walked into the room, took a cup and filled it with water from a pitcher. I pretended to type on the laptop.

"So I guess business is bad for everybody," Felix said.

"Yeah." It didn't take much to figure that out.

"It'll pick up. *La Gran Pirámide* will help. You'll see."

"I hope so," I said. We were having the same conversation again. I couldn't think of anything new to say.

He glanced at me sideways. He moved closer. That thing inside me fluttered again. I held my breath for one potato, two potatoes. Felix put his cup on the counter with a stretch and a yawn.

"I'll be back in a few days," he said. He flashed his beautiful teeth and waved goodbye. My shoulders sagged. I wanted to talk to him some more. I wanted him to stay.

CHAPTER 15

"Masi." I followed my mom's voice and climbed down the stairs that wrapped into the basement. "Masi, come here for a second," she said.

I didn't go into the basement much. I hated how small and humid it was. Except for the humidity, it wasn't at all like Colonel Franco's. It only ran about one third of the length of the bakery—no carpeting or linoleum, just concrete. There were pipes everywhere overhead which made the ceiling low. Our furnace sat at the heart.

Several dusty shelves and miscelleanous boxes lined three of the walls. A washer/dryer sat against the fourth wall with an industrial-sized two-door cabinet on one side and my dad's work bench on the other.

My eyes roamed. I spotted a great big pair of goat horns sticking out from behind a stack of boxes. I pushed the boxes aside and uncovered a pair of bicycle handlebars covered with white electrical tape. The handlebars were attached to a blue ten-speed bike—a relic. I ran my hand over it. "Nice, right? That used to be my bike," my mom said.

I turned around to look at her. She sat on the floor in front of a big red wooden box whose outside had splintered over the years. I stared. "This is my box of memories and heirlooms," she said. "Hand me one of your dad's screwdrivers. A flathead."

I grabbed a screwdriver from my dad's work bench—there were tools everywhere—and handed it over. My mom pushed the screwdriver into the top edge of the box and pried the lid off.

I leaned in. The inside was padded with a thin velvet-like material that cradled the contents. A large book covered in a plastic bag lay at the very top. My mom picked it up. "What is that?" I asked.

"A photo album. Your grandmother wants me to get her some pictures. She had some water damage during the last big storm out there. She lost a lot of her things from the old furniture store." My grandparents had owned a furniture store on the south side of the park when my mom was my age. She'd worked there as a showroom girl. My grandparents picked up and moved right after my mom married my dad. Pig Park was at its prime, and they'd done well with the sale. They lived over a thousand miles away in Texas now.

My mom tore the plastic bag off the album and flipped through it. She turned page after page. She paused at a picture of herself in a cap and gown. She held it up for me to see. "It's my high school graduation picture. Seems like a hundred years ago. Your grandfather wanted me to go to school to become an accountant."

"I didn't know that. What happened?"

"Life happened. I had other plans. I fell in love. I wanted a family." She closed the album and hugged it to herself. "I'm tired," she said. She got up and walked upstairs.

I leaned against my dad's bench. I didn't know what I wanted to be when I grew up. Most kids just grew up to work for their parents or some factory. My parents always said they just wanted me to be happy. I couldn't help wondering if my mom had secretly wanted to be an accountant too or if that was really just my grandfather's dream. It was probably better not to ask. Maybe my dad and I had gotten in my mom's way…

CHAPTER 16

"Let's go over to Peregrino's," Josefina said. I didn't know if she was serious. We had never been inside Peregrino's warehouse, and neither one of us was in the market for bulk whey protein.

"What for?" I asked.

"That's why." She pointed at a tanker-sized black SUV making its way down the street in front of us. Our reflections disappeared in a whirlpool of chrome as its rims spun by.

"Jeez." While Peregrino was the only person in Pig Park who could afford a car like that, everyone knew that he drove the warehouse van for the tax write-off. "It's not his car."

"I'm ninety-eight percent sure it was headed straight for his warehouse. Who else has rich friends?"

"Okay," I said. But I didn't care about the SUV. Felix was staying with Peregrino, and I just wanted to see him again.

Josefina and I walked to the warehouse. I hesitated going through the door. I hated being so obvious. Josefina grabbed my arm and pulled me into the building anyway.

The front room was jam-packed with boxes. They started in the hallway and sprawled out into the interior. I glanced down. Some of boxes lay open. They weren't filled with vitamins. They were crammed with clay suns and moons in various colors. There were statues of La Muerte and countless artisan skeleton figurines—riding bicycles, making dinner and walking skeleton dogs. There were also enough decorative vases and candles for Peregrino to convert his vitamin empire into a pottery store.

Felix sat at the front desk reading a book.

"What's with all the pottery?" I got to the bottom of the matter right away.

"It's just stuff my classmate brought back," Felix said.

Josefina arched a thick eyebrow. I think she was excited at the idea of a whole band of college boys. "Is that who the fancy car belongs to?" she asked.

"Yes. The truck belongs to my schoolmate. Come back and say hello." Felix waved us over to a nearby door.

A hallway connected the room to a lofted section

of the warehouse. It didn't feel like we were standing inside the same large metal building. There were beautiful wood floors, tall ceilings, fancy countertops and shiny steel appliances. It was as nice as anything in those circulars my mom got in the mail.

Josefina jabbed her elbow into me. "I guess Peregrino sold his soul a long time ago. Look at this place." She let out a soft whistle.

I couldn't help thinking the same thing. It was like in that movie *The Devil and Daniel Webster*. What did it take to get stuff that nice while everyone else was having such a hard time? Maybe it was luck—as simple as buying a lotto ticket and crossing your fingers. Or maybe you just had to pray hard enough. I pictured Peregrino sitting in his living room with thousands of lit candles, so it was nothing but fire and wax as far as the eye could see. He prayed so hard, he broke into a sweat. Then I imagined all those burning candles sending all those boxes of dieter's tea and cod liver oil tablets up in smoke. I concluded that probably wasn't how he'd gotten rich. Maybe people really did just sell their souls.

"Girls, meet Belinda. She's staying with an aunt of hers up north," Felix said. A plain thin girl with freckles and blonde hair jumped up from behind the boxes wearing an embroidered linen dress and flip-flops.

Josefina's eyebrows sunk into a half-face frown. My face wasn't doing anything better. Of course, neither of us had expected that the classmate would be a "her."

"Belinda, Masi and Josefina live in the neighborhood. They're helping build *La Gran Pirámide*," Felix said.

A smile sprawled onto Belinda's face like a lazy cat. Her face transformed. I inhaled. That sprawling smile bore witness to the power of perfect teeth. When Belinda smiled, she was beautiful.

"Would you like a glass of lemonade?" Belinda asked. She pushed a tray of lemonade-filled glasses towards us. Silver and turquoise bracelets dangled from both her wrists. "It's really good. It's made with key limes. I brought those with me too."

Josefina grabbed a glass and sipped. She stared at Belinda. Belinda smiled again and even laughed a little.

"I'm in town making deliveries for Dr. Vidales Casal," Belinda said. Her laughter wove through each sentence as if in a loop. "I'm also looking at real estate."

Felix's cat eyes sliced at her like she'd said something she shouldn't have. Belinda laughed again and charged on. She couldn't seem to stop herself. "With so little demand, there are really great deals out here."

"You're buying buildings? Boy, you must have

tons of money. You must be rich like Jorge Peregrino," Josefina said.

"No." Felix interrupted.

"My great old uncle died," Belinda said. Her laugh got even loopier. I couldn't tell if she was kidding.

"What's all the stuff in the boxes for then?"

"These girls have better things to do than spend their afternoon here. Come on, girls, I'll walk you out," Felix interrupted.

He wrapped his arm around my shoulder. Heat ran down my shoulder and up my spine. His other arm grabbed hold of Josefina. I blinked. There was no time to open my mouth again. We were outside like some kind of magic trick. He walked us all the way to the grocery store, humming softly.

I forgot all about Belinda—and even Josefina. I pretended it was just him and me. We walked to the grocery store and stopped. Felix excused himself and disappeared.

"He sure got rid of us fast. I guess he wanted to make sure we didn't stick around, spying through the windows or something," Josefina said. "I mean what do we really know about him anyway?"

"Come on." I didn't know that much, but I liked the way I felt around him. That's all I needed to know for now.

"I'm just saying."

I tuned her out. I sat on the Nowak's stairs and wondered what the devil would want in exchange for a kiss from Felix.

CHAPTER 17

The drawers knocked around. The sound was not beautiful. The knocking stopped. I dressed myself and walked into the kitchen.

My mom sat at the table with her hands clutched together tight in her lap. My dad grabbed a plate of toast with marmalade from the counter. He walked over to his armchair. He sat down. He raised the plate to his mouth, pushed half a slice in and crunched away.

"*Goooool!*" The Univision sports reporter entered endless *o* mode until a commercial came on.

Something was off. It was the silence. My parents weren't shy about letting each other have it. When I was younger, they'd fought over dumb things like the lyrics of a pop song or what to make for dinner. When the Amerian Lard Company closed down, the real arguments started. But they always worked it out.

Josefina and I argued the same way. Sometimes it was loud nonsense. Sometimes it was real. Then we were best friends again. Take, for example, the fight on top of the pyramid. The next day it'd been like nothing had ever happened.

"It's amazing how fast they put up the beams." I tried to spark a conversation. A ball of masa might've answered more readily. I shrugged, left the room and headed for Colonel Franco's. There was too much other stuff to worry about, like Belinda.

I'd spent all night turning the Belinda thing around in my head. The truth was that I was feeling jealous. The more I thought about it, the more I knew Josefina was on to something about the way Felix had shooed us away. I couldn't help wondering if Belinda was more than Felix's college friend.

I returned home after a few hours to find my mom locked in my parents' bedroom. There was no hot dinner. I finished my chores and ate a bologna sandwich. No one nagged me to eat a vegetable or anything nutritious. I squirted ketchup on my sandwich just in case. I wished it were a real dinner to comfort me, like carne asada with baked potatoes. We hadn't tasted steak in a long time on account of the cost of meat. Most of our groceries came from bartering with the Nowaks, and we ate a lot of recycled bread.

My dad walked into the room and sat down at the

table across from me. He fixed his gaze on the wall. The bedroom door opened, and my mom walked out. "Your mother is going away," my dad said.

"I'm going to go stay with your grandparents for a while," my mom said.

"Is everything okay? I mean, are they okay?" I asked.

"They're both fine. It's more of a vacation," my mom said.

I shook my head. "A vacation? We can't afford a vacation."

"I'm the only one going."

"What?"

"It's not a vacation. She just needs some time to herself," my dad said.

"It doesn't make sense for you to leave now. You're leaving like everyone else," I said. Was this seriously happening? I didn't see how she could go from being so worried about the bakery to just up and leaving.

My mom got up and headed back to the bedroom without another word. Maybe it was a practical joke. She was going to yell "Got ya" any second. I followed her and stood in front of the bedroom door. I stared at the suitcase sitting on the edge of the bed. She was serious. She grabbed face cream and deodorant from the dresser and threw them into the bag.

She looked tired, rundown.

I stomped into my room and threw myself on my bed. My mom was unhappy. It was nothing new. She complained about money an awful lot. My dad worried about money too. But she was obsessed. I lay there and wished she would just get over it, and they would work it out.

CHAPTER 18

Nothing changed overnight. There was no negotiation, not even a good-bye between my parents. After all that silence, it occurred to me that my parents didn't have much to say to each other without the arguing. The last conversation I heard between them went like this:

"Did you order the flour and sugar?"

"Yes, fifty pounds of each."

"Did you confirm delivery?"

"Yes, for Monday."

My mom picked up her suitcase. She crossed the room toward the door. Her body doubled over from the weight. My dad didn't move to help. Neither did I. I wasn't going to help her leave.

I straggled along behind her to the train stop. I thought if she saw me she might still change her mind. "You could take me with you," I said.

"Don't you think I thought about it?"

"So why don't you?"

"I know this may be your last summer with your friends. It wouldn't be fair to you," she sighed. I shook my head. "I love you and your dad very much."

"Then stay. Or just wait a few days and think about it."

"It's not that simple. The sooner I leave, the sooner I can figure things out."

I tried hard to understand why it wasn't so simple. I wanted to demand that she explain. Was it really that she needed some time away from all of this and us, like my dad said? She hugged me goodbye. I pressed my head to her shoulder and curled my fingers tight around her back.

"Everything will be alright. You'll see," she said. I wished her arms could still convince me of anything.

My dad had once told me that the morning my mom first stepped foot in the bakery he met fate. My fresh-faced mom was the most beautiful girl he had ever seen. "I'm going to grow old with Patricia Quintana," he'd said. She anchored him to Pig Park. Too bad it didn't work the other way. We couldn't hold my mom in place any more than we could hold on to the present. Or maybe we just weren't enough anymore. I thought about what she'd told me in the basement that day we looked through that old picture album. "Life happened." I wasn't any closer to understanding what that meant. You couldn't plan things? Life had a mind of its own?

My mom pulled away, picked up her suitcase, and boarded the train. The doors folded and squeezed shut. The train pushed forward. She was gone.

I pictured her on one of those faded runaway posters taped at the entrance of the train stop. The idea of my mom running away was as out there as the idea of a pyramid.

Mama birds didn't abandon their nests. But the population of stray cats proved other creatures abandoned their children easy enough. I was an orphan kitten.

I walked to Colonel Franco's. I sat at his desk typing up a letter for him. I concentrated on the keyboard. My two index fingers moved above the keys.

"My mom saw you and your mom walking outside with a suitcase," Casey said. Loretta Sanchez, Casey's mom and my mom's friend, spent all day on her stoop. Sooner or later, she knew everything.

"She left to go visit my grandparents. She hasn't seen them in a long time."

"I would've gone with her," Josefina said.

"They're getting on in their years. She wants to spend as much time with them as possible. Old people stuff. Not my thing." I didn't let on about the real situation with my mom to anyone, not even Josefina. She didn't need any more ideas about the merits of leaving.

The more I lied, the more I wished it were true.

I poured myself into a lie. My dad poured himself into the bakery. He rearranged all of the supplies and reorganized the bread in the display cases according to color while I was out.

"Dad?" I said. "Won't some of those be different colors with each batch depending on how long they stay in the oven?"

He didn't answer. I walked up to where he sat on mom's stool and waved my hand in front of his face. He was as absent as my mom. I could've put on a pig suit and walked through the house yelling: "Oink, oink." There was no talking to him. He was gone.

I finished my chores. I pulled the blinds and locked the door.

I poured two bowls of cereal. Dinner with my dad was like dinner with a cardboard box. Except the box was more interesting to read. I shoveled spoonfuls into my mouth. My dad's bowl sat untouched.

CHAPTER 19

The phone rang. I stood up and put the receiver to my right ear. There was a sound like rustling paper and tapping. "Let me talk to your dad, mijita," my grandmother said.

"He's in the bathroom." I wondered what my grandmother wanted. My mom hadn't called since leaving. "Let me talk to my mom," I said.

"Your mom is resting right now, mija. Well, I suppose I should just tell you. She fainted this afternoon."

"What?"

"She says she's just tired from the trip and refuses to call your father. It could be dehydration. She chugged a whole gallon of water when she got here. I thought she was going to swim away. She didn't want to worry you."

"I should get my dad."

"No, no. It's late. We'll see in the morning."

"Okay. Bye." My shoulders slumped.

"Who was that?" my dad asked from the doorway.

"It was my grandmother. She wanted me to tell you my mom's not feeling well. She'll call you tomorrow."

My dad didn't ask for more details, but he hovered near the phone for the rest of the night. His palm curled around the receiver a few times and then let go.

I lay in bed, staring at the ceiling. My mom probably hadn't drunk water all day. Those cross-country bus bathrooms were the worst. I hated all public bathrooms. Sometimes I didn't drink water at school for hours so that I wouldn't have to go into the girls' restroom.

Maybe the whole situation with my dad was just making my mom sick.

It occurred to me that if my mom really were sick, she'd have to come back. We didn't have some fancy health insurance plan to pay for treatment just anywhere. She'd have to come back to see a doctor at the community clinic. It's not that I hoped she was sick. But she would be forced to come back.

The phone didn't ring again until the following afternoon. My dad dove for the phone. "Yes...Yes," he uttered. His brow scrunched up. "I see...I see." He shook his head from side to side and hung up.

"Your grandmother took your mom to get checked out. Her blood sugar is high. Patricia has diabetes," he said. He spoke into the wind, as if I were in a different room.

"Diabetes?" I asked.

"She was fine when she left," he grumbled. He pulled off his apron and stormed outside. He slumped down on the front stoop.

The air squeezed out of me. Maybe I was being punished for my thoughts about my mom having to come back.

I took the phone and dialed my grandparents' number. "Mom?"

"Masi? I'm fine," my mom said. "I'm fine. The Texas Tech doctors are very capable. Your grandmother has a friend there and got me in at a reduced rate. Blood sugar problems are as common as a cold these days. Your grandmother shouldn't have said anything."

"Is that all you have to say?" I waited for her to announce that she was on her way back. But she didn't talk about returning. She babbled on about the weather as if nothing had happened.

I twirled the cord around my fingers. "Okay, I have to go." It was just one more thing I didn't know what to make of.

I looked out the front door. I walked outside and sat down beside my dad. He dragged his nails against the concrete. "I'm going down there first thing tomorrow morning," he said.

"Down where? The basement?"

"Texas."

"What about the bread?"

"It can wait. We don't have any customers anyway. You can stay with the Nowaks while I'm gone."

"Okay."

"Now go to bed."

I walked to my room. I lay on my bed, but I couldn't sleep. I listened to the radio. I read a magazine. I counted the miles to Texas and the distance to my mom's heart. I counted and counted and counted.

CHAPTER 20

I glanced at the pad with my grandmother's telephone number and dialed. "Grandma?…No, I don't need to talk to Mom. I just want to tell you that my dad boarded the first express bus out this morning. He'll be there tomorrow afternoon."

"Why'd he do that?"

"He wanted to."

"Your poor father."

"I know."

"Your mother doesn't want to go back yet."

"I guess. But she should at least listen to him. It wouldn't hurt her to come see a doctor back here."

"She's seen a doctor."

"Well, she can see another one. If not, she can tell my dad to his face when she sees him," I said and hung up. I picked up the phone and hung up a second time for good measure. My grandmother wasn't helping any. Of course, her loyalty was to the daughter she'd raised, not to the son-in-law or the grandkid she only saw every few years. She was on my mom's side all the way.

I still just wanted my mom to get on a bus home.

It didn't make any sense for her not to. I couldn't help being annoyed. I was sure she was lying about how okay it was. My dad had followed her across the country. This thing with her had to be more serious than she was letting on. There was something they weren't telling me.

I pushed the power button on the laptop. I typed the word D-I-A-B-E-T-E-S. Over one hundred and eighty million results popped up.

I deleted the letters one by one and typed F-E-L-I-X. Maybe I could get to the bottom of who Belinda was to him. I racked my brain for his last name, like pulling a splinter without tweezers. I highlighted the name and deleted. It was just as well. I didn't need something else to obsess over, as tempting as it was.

I typed D-I-A-B-E-T-E-S again. I scanned the first half a dozen sites. I clicked on one of the links. There were pictures of people with amputated limbs, people with livers that looked like my grandfather's famous Texas brisket.

A million terrible thoughts raced through my head. My eyes felt like they might pop out.

According to the website, treating diabetes was all

about a healthy diet and regular exercise. I ran upstairs and scavenged through all the cupboards in the house. I grabbed a bag of Cheetos from my dad's stash and a new bottle of hot sauce. There wasn't much else. I moved on to the refrigerator. I grabbed a sealed box of Velveeta Cheese and a three-liter bottle of orange soda. I put all of it into a paper shopping bag and set it beside the door.

I walked downstairs with the bag in hand and sat at the counter. The thing was, we ate a lot of bread. There was no way around it. I couldn't go into the bakery's pantry and clean it out too. That would be as good as throwing away money.

Maybe the bread wasn't that bad. My dad had cut out the lard from all the recipes as a matter of principle. We used vegetable shortening and butter. Nowak's grocery didn't stock American Lard products anymore either. American Lard had taken their business elsewhere and so had we.

Bang.

Click, clack.

I turned around at the rumble behind me. I walked into the kitchen and flipped the light switch on. The oven was on its last leg. It made those sounds sometimes. I put my hand over the oven door. I pressed down. The metal felt cold against my palm.

I was losing my mind.

I dug my hands into my scalp. I was ready to tear my hair out. Each thought that followed was worse, as if being alone were a magnifying glass of bad feelings. I didn't want to cry, but what if my mom's liver turned to brisket? Maybe she would never come back.

CHAPTER 21

I pulled on my backpack and grabbed the shopping bag. I stepped out and locked the door. Clouds hovered and swallowed up the sky.

I ran the block and a half to the Nowaks' in the ominous dark. It was too early for streetlights. My shoulders shook. The clouds sprayed their fury—each raindrop heavier than the last—and hot tears gushed down my face. I gulped down the warm damp air. I pushed through the side door of the grocery store and climbed the stairs to Josefina's room.

Josefina turned off the TV.

"What's the matter?" she asked. She pulled up her desk chair.

"My mom left. They're not even talking to each other. I think they broke up. We found out she was sick. My dad followed her." It spilled out like soup left to boil over.

"Grownups don't break up. What do you mean she's sick?"

I wiped at my face and told Josefina all about the blowout at home and the diabetes. "I don't understand why this is happening now, as if everything else wasn't bad enough."

"Your mom will be okay. They'll figure it out." Josefina handed me a towel. I dried off and changed into my pajamas. I hung my damp clothes on her desk chair. "Everything will work out, you'll see," she said.

"What's going on here?" Marcos asked from the doorway.

"Go back to your room," Josefina said. "Get out of here."

I smiled a little. Their family seemed so normal next to mine: brothers and sisters fighting, parents who lived together. I wouldn't have minded permanently moving in with the Nowaks.

Josefina turned the television back on Marcos walked in and sat on the floor. "What are we watching?" he asked.

"Go away," Josefina repeated.

"I don't mind if he stays," I said. I looked for comfort in the familiarity of Marcos. I pulled out the bag of Cheetos I'd brought with me and tossed it and the orange soda his way. Marcos drank the soda straight from the bottle.

"Look, Masi," he said. He stuffed his face with two fistfuls of the crunchy chips so that his cheeks puffed out. I laughed a little.

"You're the spitting image of that squirrel that hangs out outside my window at night."

"I turn into a squirrel when you're not looking," he smiled. Like I said, sometimes he was nice.

"Marcos!" Mrs. Nowak yelled from the other room.

"Fun's over," Marcos said and left.

Josefina grabbed me by the arm and led me downstairs to the store. "We're gonna help your mom get better," she said. She put a basket in my hands and walked past the deli section. She threw in a can of non-fat cooking spray, Splenda, canola oil, yogurt, unsweetened applesauce, and various vegetables. She bagged the groceries and we walked back upstairs.

"Felix told my parents he was going to the bakery tomorrow. You should go tell him your dad is gone," she said.

"I don't know."

"It'll help you get your mind off things. I'll go with you."

"Maybe you're right. But you were all weird about him last time."

"Just because I'm not interested anymore, doesn't mean you can't be. I'll be nice. I promise."

"I don't remember his last name."

"Diaz, I believe."

"Diaz." I repeated, as if to engrave it on my mind.

"I looked him up," she said. "A million hits, none of them Felix. Weird, but better than finding out he's a murderer."

Josefina lay down on her bed. She turned off the light. I lay down next to her. I watched the shadows of her ceiling fan grow big and small, going round and round.

She rolled over and sighed.

I wondered if she was thinking about Otto, the boy who had moved away. Sometimes things didn't work out. They didn't work out at all. I could accept it for what it was or trip and fall into a gloom. If I looked at everyone around me—if I looked at Josefina and Otto, if I looked at my mom and my dad—then love didn't last. But I didn't want to be like my mom or Josefina. I didn't want to give up on friendship, Pig Park, or love.

I drew a blanket around myself and closed my eyes.

CHAPTER 22

Josefina pushed the door of the bakery open. A sour smell that reminded me of the bottom of a clothes hamper hit us. I'd left a tray of bolillos out the day before. The warm weather and yeast had worked their dark magic.

I walked in and threw my keys on the counter. I drew the shades and opened the windows a crack to let the fresh air in.

"Wow," Josefina said. "It stinks in here. Should we do something?"

"Let's sort out the good pieces of bread and toast them for capirotada," I said.

"Good idea. Does it matter that it's not Lent?"

"I don't think so. It's better than throwing everything away." According to my dad, people ate capirotada during Lent because the bread represented the Body of Christ. The syrup was his blood. The raisins on top were the nails, and the cinnamon sticks were the wood of the cross. Religious purpose aside, it also tasted good.

I sorted whatever pieces of bread felt soft and sniffed them to make sure they were still edible.

Josefina walked into the kitchen. She grabbed a saucepan and filled it with water. She waited for it to boil and added two cinnamon sticks and a cylinder of raw cane sugar. We watched the sugar melt into syrup. I sliced the salvaged pieces of bread and arranged them on a tray. I turned on the oven, though I didn't know if I could trust it, and pushed the tray in to toast the bread. I turned the pantry inside out until I found the raisins. I sighed.

"Are you thinking about your parents again?" Josefina asked.

"I'm not." I was only thinking about my mom. My dad was upset, but he was not sick. I moved the stool in front of the counter—my mom's favorite place to sit while she waited for customers who never came.

I tidied up the ransacked kitchen and tried not to think about anything.

A few minutes passed.

Someone rapped against the window. I looked up to see a head of hair rollers. Loretta Sanchez pressed her big round face close to the glass. "Hope your mom feels better, mija," she said in that loud voice of hers.

"I'll be sure to tell her you said so." I called back. She somehow already knew about my mom being sick.

She smiled, dismissed us with a nod and moved on to her next order of business.

I spread butter across the top sides of the toast.

The next knock on the window came from Felix. Josefina hurried and opened the door for him.

"I heard about your mom. I ran into Loretta outside," he said to me. I shrugged. Although I felt like yelling at Loretta for broadcasting my family's private business, I wasn't going to let it ruin my afternoon with Felix.

"What are you girls making?" Felix asked.

"We're making capirotada with the stale bread," I answered, stumbling on my words. Every nerve in my body was trying to edge out of my skin. Meanwhile, Felix was cool and calm. There wasn't a hair out of place or a breath out of rhythm.

"Cool. You know why bread goes stale?"

"Because it's old?" Josefina said.

"It's a chemical reaction. Bread has high levels of starch, which crystallizes in cool temperatures. The process is called retrogradation. The formation of crystals leaves the bread hard. The same thing happens when you leave bread out in room temperature—the bread comes into contact with bacteria in the air," he explained. We nodded politely. It was all 'blagity-blah, blah, blah,' but I couldn't tear my eyes from his lips.

I could smell him. He smelled of campfire. I imagined that's what all of New Mexico smelled like. I breathed in slow, holding his scent. I realized what I was doing, and the heat climbed from my chest up to my scalp. I looked away.

I hurried back to the kitchen. Felix and Josefina followed. I layered the buttered bread onto a pan and added pecans. "Sprinkle these on." I put a box of raisins on the counter. Felix's hand hovered two inches from mine. He picked up the box and sprinkled the raisins. I topped our creation with grated cheese, poured the syrup over it, and pushed the pan into the oven. We each grabbed a fork while Josefina poured milk into three cups. The cheese melted—the capirotada was ready. It was gooey—and smelled as good as the boy next to me.

Felix's portion disappeared in two bites. "This is quite wonderful," he said. I hadn't even picked up my fork. My hand was tense at my side. I was too close to him. I didn't want anything getting caught between my teeth or dribbling down my shirt.

"Have you had this before?" I asked.

"Not like this." His lips curved into a smile. He rubbed his belly. "I should get going."

"You want to take some with you?"

"That's a good idea," Josefina said.

Felix's eyes opened wide and he nodded. "It's nothing but canned soup over at Jorge Peregrino's. Not that I'm complaining. I grew up on ramen. My mother worked a lot. Variety is very welcome, that's all."

I prepared a plastic container for him. I wrapped up the rest to take back to the Nowaks. Josefina pulled the shades.

"Thanks for everything, Masi," Felix said. I mustered half a wave, sorry to see him walk away again.

CHAPTER 23

I looked at the door. My dad and I stood in the middle of the bakery. Neither of us said a thing. I didn't bother him with any bakery updates. He didn't notice the pillaging of the cupboards. The oven groaned. "Back to work." He dismissed me with a wave.

"And Mom?"

"Your mother refused to come back with me."

I kicked myself for asking. My grandmother had said she wouldn't come. Then there was nothing as obvious as my dad walking through that door alone. I didn't know what to say. I limped away with my foot in my mouth.

My dad stayed put by the counter. Bloodshot eyes gazed out the window. The phone rang. I reached over him and grabbed the phone next to the counter.

"Masi?"

"Mom."

"Masi."

"What are you doing, Mom?" I asked.

"I'm reading a book in the backyard." My grandparents' Spanish-style home had a rose-colored terracotta tile patio and a yard the size of half a city block. All around them were mountains. They'd figured out a way to make the money from the sale of their furniture store stretch. "It's a gardening book. Your grandmother promised to show me how to grow geraniums, gardenias and pecans. She has a tree out here that she grew herself from a pecan. Can you believe that? I mean, I grew up a city girl like you. Your grandmother on the other hand came from a whole different world. She thrives here. I think I'm starting to thrive here too."

"No, I mean what are you planning to do?" I asked.

"Oh, I'll be helping your grandmother in the kitchen. She wants to hand dry her homegrown chilies for chilaquiles. You should see how beautiful they are. We're also waking up at five in the morning tomorrow to make pozole."

It wasn't what I meant either. She didn't get it. She was sick. She needed to come home. She needed to stop eating fried tortillas and pork. She needed to start being a mom.

I didn't say anything. She hadn't come back after

my dad had gone all the way there. She wasn't coming back on account of anything I said. I wasn't going to nag her the way she did my dad about money or me about picking up after myself. She was a grown-up. I guessed she could take care of herself.

"I should get to bed now. I'm a little tired. Even with the time difference, I have to get up with the roosters tomorrow," she said.

"Hold on a second." I put the hand over the receiver and pushed the phone in my dad's direction.

He pushed it back and stomped out of the room.

"Sorry, I was checking to see if dad was here. He's not."

"That's fine. I'm going to bed. My mouth is watering just thinking about those chilaquiles."

"Goodnight then," I said. I hung up the phone. My mom annoyed me plenty of times, but now I was also getting angry. I was angry at her for the first time since she'd thrown away my favorite T-shirt claiming I'd outgrown it. I loved that thing.

I threw my hands up in the air. Let her stuff her face with fried tortillas. I didn't care what that meant for my dad either. Maybe they would get a divorce.

Happily ever after had turned into happily never after, but people split all the time. Casey and Stacey didn't have a dad and neither did Iker or Felix. I wouldn't have a mom. I didn't like it, but I would learn to live with it.

I needed for Pig Park to be saved and for Josefina to stick around more than ever.

CHAPTER 24

My dad crouched down and stuffed the display case with croissants, rolls, and ginger pigs. He was in the same T-shirt and jeans he'd worn the night before. "Baked some bread," he said.

"I'm going to Colonel Franco's for a few hours," I said. Sitting in Colonel Franco's basement was better than thinking about my mom. At least there was still hope for Pig Park.

I glanced at the bakery counter later that afternoon. There were three more trays of rolls stacked on top. "You're still baking? Did we get an order or something?" I asked.

"I just felt like baking."

The bread wasn't going anywhere.

It was too much for capirotada or croutons. I pulled out clear plastic Ziploc bags, and filled them to try and keep the bread fresh longer.

My dad pounded more masa. He slid two additional trays into the oven.

The phone rang. It was my mom. "We're kind of in the middle of something," I said. I didn't tell her anything else. I was a little embarrassed for my dad. Maybe I was a little scared too.

I opened my eyes wide and closed them at the sight of the counter the next morning. One, two, three, four, five, six, seven more trays of bread. I filled more bags and stuffed them in the cupboards. I set them on top of the refrigerator, on the table, and even on the dining room chairs. The piles grew and grew. He cranked out batch after batch.

My dad had finally lost it. I wanted to scream that he'd gone insane, but I pursed my lips into a tight line.

I took a few dozen ginger pigs and croissants to the Nowaks. "My dad overdid it with the bread. He's been baking all night. There's piles of bread everywhere," I said to Josefina.

"Why did he do that?" she asked.

"Maybe it helps him keep his mind off my mom. Can I borrow one of the grocery store carts so I can haul it away?"

"Sure. Marcos!" she yelled. "Can you bring a cart out for Masi?"

Marcos pulled a cart out into the street for me. "Where are you taking it?" he asked.

"I'm still trying to figure that part out."

"I can help you push it."

"It's okay. Thanks anyway, Marcos."

I pushed the cart to the bakery, racking my mind for a solution. I parked the cart out front and walked into the bakery. Then it came to me. "I'm taking these leftovers to the church," I said. Maybe I could pray to God while I was at it.

I grabbed an armful of bags and kicked the door open with my foot. I tripped on the threshold, dropping some of the bags.

"Too much for capirotada, huh?" my dad said. He picked up the bags off the ground and slung them over his shoulder. He stood there. I stood there. I realized that he meant to come with me. I just about tripped again.

I glanced across the street at the park. Red, yellow and brown bricks peaked through the trees. With everything going on, I'd barely noticed that the pyramid walls had started going up.

We cut across the alley and entered the church. It was a chapel attached to the west building of the American Company. The pews were empty. I headed to the back room. "Father Arturo?" I called to its sole holdout.

Father Arturo was typing away on his computer.

He swiveled his chair a half circle to face us. "Come in, come in, hijos."

"We brought bread," my dad said from behind me. "It's a lot. Where should we put it?"

"Such generosity, Masi and Tomás! Come, come." Father Arturo led us to a table along the wall outside his office. "This will be a wonderful gift for my weekly visit with the missionaries. They can really use this." With so few God-fearing people left in Pig Park, Father Arturo spent most of the week at other parishes.

We placed the bags on the table.

"I'll catch up with you at home," my dad said. He plopped down in one of the back pews. I'd meant to stick around, but I walked away without asking and gave my dad his space. I acted like it was the kind of thing that happened every day.

My dad walked in through the front door of the bakery about an hour later. He stood taller. He rested his bread-kneading fists on his hips. "I'm winning back your mother," he said. He smiled with his entire face so that his eyes crinkled at the corners. I would always think of that as the look of salvation.

CHAPTER 25

My dad pounded down the ball of masa with his knuckles. His moment of craziness had passed so I went back to thinking about other things.

"I forgot to tell you. Felix was looking for you while you were gone. We spent the morning making capirotada, but he probably wants to talk business," I said.

"I should call him and ask him over then," my dad said. It worked better than if I'd planned it.

Felix walked in later that afternoon. "Hi, Masi."

"Hi, Felix."

"Is your dad here?"

"Yes." I pointed to the back from my spot at the register.

My dad burst out of the kitchen with a pot of coffee in one hand. "Felix, glad to see you. I completely forgot we were meeting last week. Good thing this daughter of mine is on top of it and you were able to reschedule. I made some coffee. Have some bread."

"Thank you so much. It's really not necessary."

"No need for shyness here." My dad put a mug and a ginger pig on the counter. Then he poured the coffee. Felix tore at the ginger pig's soft brown flesh until it was gone. He picked a large crumb off his shirt and put it in his mouth.

"Mmmm, as delicious as everything else. Okay, now to our business. The goal is to help you make your bakery as inviting as possible for when *La Gran Pirámide* is finished," Felix said.

"When the bakery first opened," my dad began, "the bread sold itself. Our product was pure and simple. People bought food to eat, absolutely no other reason. No gimmicks. Those were different times."

My dad told Felix about his dreams as a young man—about the journey to the heartland, before Pig Park and my mom, before the wheat and life took their toll. The first few years were hard, but nothing like this. Once he and abuelita Carmelita got the bakery going, the American Lard Company's influx of workers meant that business boomed. Their sacrifices paid off.

The trip down memory lane had my dad sounding like his old self again.

"Your mother must have been a great woman," Felix said.

"That is very kind of you, Felix. With all the work

you do for Dr. Vidales Casal, I expect you've heard your share of stories."

"I've heard a thing or two, but I only started working for him this summer. I'm getting credit and a stipend to work off part of my tuition so my mom doesn't have to. I don't like her to worry about how much school costs. She waits tables. She's on her feet all day. She already works hard."

"I'm sure she's very proud of you, Felix." My dad topped off the coffee mugs. "I'll be honest, Felix. I'm not good at all these types of things. I'm only good at one thing: making bread. I'm not sure how to do what you're asking for."

"I think maybe you don't give yourself enough credit. Just think of it as making your business stand out."

"I bet Masi would be more helpful than me. Masi, you can come up with some ideas, right?"

"Sure," I said. Although I wasn't really so sure.

"Sounds like a plan. I have to meet Mr. Wong this afternoon, but I'll come back tomorrow so we can talk about it some more." Felix downed the remains of his cup and left.

I climbed the stairs to my room. Laundry lay neglected and festering in piles by the door. I kicked a few shirts aside. There was a notebook somewhere.

I found it on the other side of my bed under a scarf. I pulled the notebook up to my nose and sniffed it. It smelled of vanilla. It smelled of my mom.

Even though I had said I was done worrying about my mom, I couldn't help thinking about her.

I picked up the phone and dialed my grandparents' number. I wanted to hear her voice. I wanted to tell her she was selfish and that she had nearly broken my dad. "Where's the laundry detergent?" I asked instead.

"It's in the basement cabinet next to the washing machine," she said. I hung up. I knew exactly where it was, but I couldn't bring myself to say what I wanted to say. I took the notebook and a pencil downstairs with me to the basement. I tried to brainstorm ideas while the washer ran to keep my mind off my mom. No ideas entered my head.

I glanced at my mom's bike. I pulled it out of the basement, dusted it off, pumped air in the tires, and rode around in circles. Then I rode by the warehouse. Finally I rode to the Nowak Grocery Store where I found Josefina sprawled on the front stoop. "What are you doing with a bicycle?"

"Exercise," I said. It sounded good enough. "Listen, I need your help. My dad wants me to come up with ideas to make us look more attractive to visitors."

"Wash your face."

"I'm serious."

"Yeah, yeah. My parents are coming up with ideas too. They haven't asked for help, so I got plenty of extra ideas to spare." She sat silent for several minutes.

"So? What are all your spare ideas?"

"Hmmmn, sell dog cookies."

"That makes about as much sense as building a pyramid in the middle of Pig Park."

"Very funny. No, listen. You can just add it to the stuff Burciaga's already makes. People with money love to pay for things they don't need. There's no other way to explain truffles and charter flights to the moon. Dogs will eat their own poop, but people will pay for dog cookies."

"You're nuts." How did she come up with these things?

"Your dad can make a canine version of your pastries. You can sell Burciaga's dog T-shirts and let people come in with their dogs to pick out their favorite treat."

"The health code inspectors will have a field day with that." I'd never even been allowed to have a pet. "Well, what if we got people T-shirts? We could get nice shirts made for us with our name embroidered on them. We'll look more professional. I'm going home to tell my dad." I pedaled away.

"That's fine too," she yelled from the stoop. "Maybe."

CHAPTER 26

My dad and Felix sat on the stools in front of the counter. I hovered at arm's length. My right foot tap-danced. I grabbed the coffee pot handle and poured coffee into their mugs, stirring in evaporated milk and sugar.

I didn't want Felix to think that I was just some dumb kid. Of course, I still longed for my mom to come back, but there wasn't much I could do. I finally had a chance to make a real difference this summer. Maybe I could actually help save the bakery and Pig Park. Josefina would have to stick around. No more licking envelopes.

"Masi, tell Felix what you told me," my dad said.

I put the coffee pot back in its place and picked up the sugar bowl. The spoon clinked against the porcelain. I clasped my forefinger around it. "I thought we could order shirts with the bakery's name and our names embroidered on them. It would make us look more professional."

Felix scribbled into his notebook. "That's fantastic. See. I knew you'd have something good."

"Thank you." I stood a little straighter and felt more at ease. I hadn't made a fool of myself.

"What happens now?" my dad asked.

"I'm going to finish talking to all of the businesses. There's a neighborhood meeting in a week. I'll present everyone's ideas there. That'll be your chance to come together and discuss which suggestions the larger group can also benefit from."

"Are you nervous?"

Felix chuckled. "Only a little."

My dad laughed too. Their laughter rang in my ears. I put the sugar and milk away. I grabbed a dish rag and wiped down the counters. I tuned out the rest of the conversation.

The boys had made a great deal of progress with the pyramid. I thought about what Pig Park would be like with all those new people coming. Maybe they wouldn't all be new. Maybe some of the old Pig Park residents like Otto would return. That would make Josefina happy. It would be like the American Lard Company never left. They would even reopen our old school.

"Masi," my dad called. I woke up from the daydream. "Grab the computer when you're done. Felix is going to show you some websites."

I pulled the laptop from its drawer and waited for

it to turn on. My dad pushed his stool back. The metal legs scraped against the floor. He excused himself into the kitchen.

Felix leaned into the computer. His campfire smell hung in the air. I held my breath. I giggled for no reason at all.

Felix got closer and typed something. "There," he said. "This is a good site for supplies. It's affordable, and they offer free shipping. Never pay for shipping."

"Okay," I said. "How do you know all this anyway?"

"Experience."

"But you're smart too."

"Well, they didn't let me skip a few grades for nothing. Just kidding. My mom pushed for that. I wanted to stay with my friends in the fourth grade. I guess it worked out. I'll get out of school faster and be able to work sooner."

"Is college hard?" I asked. No one I knew had gone away to college. They'd just gone away.

His eyes focused on the computer screen as he typed in a different web address. "There's one more website… College is work, but if you work hard you'll do well. You're smart too. You don't seem afraid of work either."

I reached for the laptop to look at the website he pulled up. My hand brushed his. I let it to sit there. He smiled. The corners of my mouth pushed up against my cheeks.

"She had straight A's at American Academy. She was top of her class," my dad said from behind us.

I jumped back and stuck my hand in my pocket. "It was a small school," I said. I looked away feeling a little embarrassed.

"She's a modest one. It was the best charter school in the city," my dad said. "Anyway, don't mind me. I'm just walking through. Have a good night, Felix."

Felix gazed across the room out the window. "I should get going too. I didn't realize how late it was."

My dad followed Felix to the front door. "Felix, when you have a chance, I have another project you might be able to help with. We can test your chemistry chops," he said.

Felix smiled and nodded. "Sure thing." He waved goodbye to me and took off.

My dad locked the door and disappeared upstairs

I smiled at the thought of our hands touching. All this face-to-face with Felix meant I had something new to obsess about. The phone rang one, two...six times. I ignored it.

CHAPTER 27

I hadn't slept all night just thinking about the neighborhood meeting. Would Felix tell everyone about my idea? My stomach was a knot. I changed three times before pulling on a T-shirt and pair of shorts straight from the dryer.

"Ready?" I asked my dad. He rolled his eyes and laughed. "What?"

"I've been standing by the door for half an hour." I pinched his arm. He laughed even harder until I was laughing too, and there were tears in our eyes.

We cut through the park and paused. I stared at the pyramid. Its mismatch of brick and protruding corners had now reached the top. It really was as magnificent as one those sculptures downtown. "Wow."

"Wow," my dad repeated. He stopped and looked at it as if we were seeing it for the first time. He probably was. He'd probably never stopped to look at it before. I felt the same sense of awe. I wanted to pat myself on the back, even though I'd had such a small part in it.

We arrived at Wong's Taco Shop a few minutes before Felix's presentation. "Tomás," Colonel Franco said. My dad sat next to him. I took a chair next to Josefina and Marcos.

"Almost the moment of truth," I said. I glanced at Felix a few chairs down. Belinda sat next to him. She smoothed her crisp white shirt and blue slacks. She pushed a few runaway wisps of hair into the bun on the back of her head and away from her face.

"She cleans up good," Marcos said. I elbowed him hard.

Belinda leaned into Felix and whispered something. Felix flashed his beautiful teeth. I thought back to how he had called me smart. But Belinda was a college girl. She knew things I didn't. I looked away.

"She's not going to disappear just because you looked away," Josefina said. She smiled sympathetically, in that way I'd grown used to since the day we'd walked into kindergarten together. I shrugged.

The gathering wasn't so different from the one where Peregrino had revealed Dr. Vidales Casal's pyramid idea. Felix moved to the front of the room and cleared his throat. He waited for everyone to sit down.

"Welcome," he said. "I've had the pleasure of speaking to all of you individually. I am very excited to talk about how we can make sure this neighborhood project works for all of you. There is nothing simple about it, but we are going to make sure your project is a success. You have collectively contributed many wonderful ideas. Some I think really only apply to your respective businesses, but there are TWO ideas that we can all start thinking about and apply. My classmate Belinda has worked extensively with Dr. Vidales Casal and played a large role in the Zochimilco of Minnesota project. With no further ado, Belinda will go over our plan this morning."

Belinda walked to the front of the room with a water bottle in hand.

"Good morning, Belinda," someone in the back said.

"Good morning, everyone," Belinda said. "Please just listen and hold your comments until we've covered all of our points. Let me start off by saying that I am honored to be here. Felix has told me a great deal about what's happening and you should be truly proud." She laughed her loopy laugh and gulped down her water. "FIRST: Many of you have expressed concern about whether people will come, have a look, and go on their way. It doesn't have to play out that way. We can make it so that people want to stop and really take it all in. We can turn *La Gran Pirámide* into a museum or gallery of sorts. We can put replicas of historical artifacts in the pyramid, replicate glyphs on the walls, that sort of thing. This means you will now have to work extra hard to also get the inside of the pyramid finished by mid August.

"SECOND: We will market your neighborhood as festive. We'll promote and celebrate the pyramid's unveiling, Día de los Muertos, posadas, Cinco de Mayo. All the businesses will put up altars for Day of the Dead. That will give people reasons to come, and your businesses can use the foot traffic to bring in serious money."

"How are we going to pay to finish the inside of *La Gran Pirámide*, let alone buy all these things you're talking about? I sold my car just to pay for the other part of this." Mr. Wong said.

"He's right. I already put every last cent I had left on this," Loretta said. "Besides, we don't celebrate Cinco de Mayo. That's just for people who like to get drunk. Don't get me started on Day of the Dead. It's disrespectful to try to make money off of our dead. And where are we supposed to get all these 'historical' artifacts? Are we supposed to make people think they're real? Are we building a museum now? I just stood here with my mouth shut last time because we are all so desperate, but not this time."

"You have concerns. That's valid," interrupted that voice from the back. Peregrino slithered out of the shadows. It was only the second time I'd seen him all summer, even after going to his home. "There are a dozen empty storefronts lining the street. Those businesses couldn't stay open when the neighborhood changed. You have to change with Pig Park or the same will happen to you. These young people are trying to help. You found a way to build *La Gran Pirámide*. What more are a few walls? Dr. Vidales Casal had the foresight to send Belinda with boxes to help adorn it. Listen to her. Give her a chance." Peregrino enunciated every syllable in each word carefully. Felix nodded in agreement.

The purpose of the boxes in Peregrino's warehouse revealed itself. None of it was what I'd expected. I almost forgot about my T-shirt idea. I took a long slow look around the room. My eyes connected with my dad's. He shrugged.

The room exploded again.

"It could take days just to get the plans revised," Loretta said.

"It won't take days. I'll work as fast as I can. This isn't

exactly a bridge. But I, for one, am not ready to give up now," Colonel Franco said.

"He's right. But everyone has to be willing to try," my dad said. People looked around the room. They argued back and forth for what felt like hours until one person shook their head up and down, then another, and another, and everyone was in agreement.

Peregrino swelled like a peacock. "It's decided then," he said. The crowd dispersed in their separate directions. Marcos and the boys headed for the park. I walked to Colonel Franco's basement with Josefina.

I glanced at the pyramid.

"This is crazy," Josefina said to me.

"That never stopped us before," I said.

I couldn't say it enough. At the very least, this new project meant we would get to spend some more of the summer together—even after the outside walls of the pyramid were done. Maybe it was also our ticket to working outside once and for all. Never mind about the details.

CHAPTER 28

Colonel Franco slapped ten sealed packs of colored tissue paper and one ream of white copier stock onto the table. "I'm going to teach you how to make papel picado," he said.

He set a chair next to us, eyes focused, as if he were about to teach us the art of war.

He pulled out a tissue square with the care of someone detonating a bomb. There were images of skeletons on bicycles perforated into the paper. "You will create a series of similar squares to string together. The papel picado will hang like party streamers at *La Gran Pirámide*'s unveiling and the other celebrations we talked about."

"Can't we just go to the party store to get regular party streamers?" Casey asked.

"No, papel picado is a long-honored tradition."

He laid down a sheet of copy paper and placed a couple of layers of tissue paper on top. He folded it into a paper taco and scored the outer paper with a pencil. He took a pair of scissors and executed a series of small quick cuts along the folded edges.

"Depending on your design, you can fold the paper several more times before cutting. Remember three things." He snipped away. "Plan your design. You can't erase a cut. Be careful when pulling the paper apart. Tissue paper is very fragile." He pulled the paper apart and revealed three skulls cut into the square.

"Boy, you must've been the Martha Stewart of the barracks," I said.

"I wasn't always a soldier, girls. I'm heading out to set the boys up. I expect to see some progress when I return." He stood up and left.

I tried to concentrate on the task. Thoughts of Felix invaded. I cut out the name Felix and then quickly hacked my tissue paper to pieces.

"I saw that," Josefina said.

She cut out a silhouette of a pig's head that looked half decent, but nowhere near as good as Colonel Franco's handiwork. The best I came up with was a cutout of a pyramid. It didn't look any harder than making paper snowflakes, but it was. It was the kind of thing it would take a day just to learn and Colonel Franco hadn't been very thorough with his teaching.

It took many failed attempts to get even a few usable pieces. We folded and glued the top edges of the finished pieces over string. We spaced the pieces a few inches apart to create a flag effect.

I sliced my fingers twice: once with the scissors, the second time on the edge of the copy paper. "We better go ask Colonel Franco for bandaids," Josefina said. We ran out to the park to find him.

A series of four-by-fours sat propped along the exterior of the pyramid. The frame had built in studholes, but with all those angles, maybe it seemed impossible. Colonel Franco and the boys stood there and stared at the puzzle pieces.

A paleta man had set up across the street making a business of it all.

"Let's not interrupt them. It's stopped bleeding," I said. I held up my fingers. "Let's go back."

"No, let's stay for a while."

Josefina walked over to the paleta man and returned with a treat for us both. We lapped at the mango and milk popsicles and watched Colonel Franco and the boys.

"Go back inside," Colonel Franco commanded when he caught sight of us standing around. "And, don't get that stuff on the paper."

We returned to the basement and arrived just in time

for a full-blown stare-down between Casey and Stacey. They were like two beasts straight out of the Animal Planet. Casey dragged her chair across the room, away from Stacey, and next to us. Stacey collected all of the discarded paper and cut it into tiny bits until there was a large mound of confetti in front of her.

"Quit it," I said.

"I'm sick of her acting like a baby," Casey said.

"I've had it with her bossing me around," Stacey said over her.

Stacey pushed herself up in a huff and stood behind Casey. She held her fists over Casey's head. Instead of pounding down, she showered handfuls of confetti on her, like it was New Years or Easter or something. The humidity had softened the product in Casey's hair, so the confetti stuck to her head like a paper mache helmet.

"Oooh," Casey yelled. She stood with her knees slightly bent, a lioness about to pounce. I don't know why, but I picked up the large glue bottle. Josefina closed her eyes and shook her head. I mustered all my strength, and flung it across the room. It hit the wall and burst on contact. Glue splattered all over: on the furniture, on our arms, on our hair, on our clothes.

Josefina's eyes opened wide, and she stared at me. No words.

Stacey reached out and grabbed more confetti with both her fists and flung it into the air. The rest of us followed suit.

It rained confetti.

Colonel Franco walked in on us. He put his two fingers between his lips and let loose a human car horn.

We stopped. There was complete silence.

He cracked a smile. "Looks like you guys broke the piñata without me," he said. The room exploded into laughter. "Since we've already begun the celebration, this is as good a time as any to tell you that I've decided I'm moving you back outside so you can help the boys with the walls. You start on Monday. Clean up in here before you leave."

I applauded. Working outside with the boys couldn't possibly be any less hazardous than an unsupervised basement. Casey and Stacey would get some space from each other. Josefina and I would get some sunshine. The boys would get some real help.

My face felt like it was about to split in half.

CHAPTER 29

Felix double tied a green apron around his waist and pulled on rubber gloves. A pair of goggles sat strapped to his head. Unfamiliar packages of powder and small brown bottles lay scattered across the counter.

He crouched down to eye level with the packages. His eyes searched for something. He looked up, and his lips parted into a smile. I smiled back.

My dad pushed through the kitchen door wearing a matching pair of goggles. "Felix is helping me with a new recipe for molasses."

"Why would you need a recipe for molasses? It's simple. You just take the piloncillo and melt it in a little water." I picked up one of the small hard cylinders of cane sugar.

"This is a little different," Felix said. "Come back here. We'll show you."

I put down the cylinder of sugar and followed them into the kitchen. The stovetop was lined with saucepans full of a dark substance in varying degrees of muddiness. It looked like genuine weird science.

"Want to taste it?"

"I'll pass. Nice goggles, by the way," I said. "I won't even ask why you're wearing those."

"We won't ask anything either," my dad said and pointed at my arms.

I looked down at my arms and remembered the glue and confetti. "Excuse me," I said and hurried upstairs.

I grabbed a loofah from the cabinet under the sink and jumped in the shower. I closed my eyes and let the hot water run over me. I scrubbed at the glue until I could see the cherry hues under the bark of my skin. I wrapped a supersized towel that felt softer than my own skin around myself.

There was a chaos of unfolded laundry on my bed. I pulled out and put on a pair of jeans and a tank top. I thought back to Colonel Franco's announcement. The idea of returning to the park made me skip all the way down the stairs to tell Felix and my dad.

My dad was already clearing the counter and putting the packages away. I searched the kitchen, then the front room. "Where's Felix?" I asked.

"He had to leave." He locked the door.

"Oh." My shoulders slumped. I walked back into the

kitchen and rinsed out the saucepans, scraping at the gunk. "Why are there only two dirty trays?"

"I've cut our inventory down to bolillos and marranitos until *La Gran Pirámide* opens. It'll help us save money on supplies."

"That makes sense," I said.

My dad sat down at the counter with his little recipe box and flipped through the cards inside. It was the box he kept tucked away in his wardrobe like a treasure. It was the same one he and abuelita Carmelita had carried away with them when the old baker passed away.

The phone rang once, twice, three times.

"I thought you guys were making up. Shouldn't you answer the phone and talk to her?"

"Soon," he said. He smiled. He didn't tear his eyes away from the cards. I couldn't help wondering what he was planning in his quest to win my mom back.

I picked up the phone even though I still grew more upset with her each day she didn't come back. "Yes, Mom. We're all doing fine. How are you?…my grandparents?…Hmmm, that's good…Me too. Bye." I set the phone down.

My dad picked up a pencil and scribbled a few things on one of the cards. "Felix is a really smart kid. I told him about this idea I have, and he's been helping with it."

"That's good, Dad."

"You should talk to him," he said. "I mean, have a real conversation with him. He's a good boy."

"Really, Dad." It wasn't like I hadn't thought about it. I found myself thinking about Felix more and more. Only I didn't think about talking—I thought about his lips and his suffocating eyes.

CHAPTER 30

The morning sun shone down on Felix, tinting his eyes the color of honey. I unlocked the door and let him in.

"Good morning, Masi," he said.

"Good morning."

"Is your dad here?"

"He'll be out in a minute."

"Okay."

"Can I ask you something? Why didn't Dr. Vidales Casal just put you in charge? You've been here from the beginning. I mean we don't really need Belinda." The question had just popped into my head.

"Belinda is very capable. She's known Dr. Vidales Casal her whole life and learned everything from him."

"Her whole life? How is that even possible?"

"She's his daughter." My eyes opened wide. Felix shook his head. "I wasn't supposed to say that. Please don't repeat it."

"Why?"

"It's her personal business. Besides, it's not the only reason she's here."

I nodded. It explained why we were supposed to listen to her. It also explained the nice car and the look of money.

My dad walked in with a fresh pot of coffee, putting an end to the conversation. He poured Felix a cup. Felix grabbed the evaporated milk and sugar.

I watched them perform their morning ritual.

My dad sat down and brought his cup of coffee to his face. "Felix, I've been thinking about something. There's no such thing as Cinco de Mayo bread, but there is such a thing as Día de los Muertos bread. We don't always make it, I suppose, because we rarely celebrate it. Do you and your mom celebrate it back home?"

"Not that I can remember."

"We celebrated Día de los Muertos back in my hometown, but we never have here. I haven't made the bread in years. People honor their dead on All Saints Day and All Souls Day by going to the cemetery or setting up altars at home. The bread is sweet because everyone loves sweets. People leave it out like cookies for Santa to draw the spirits of their loved ones back for the night."

"I bet it's delicious."

"We can make a batch if you have time, Felix," my dad offered.

He washed his hands and grabbed the anise from the cupboard. He melted together warm butter, milk and water. He measured out the flour and combined it with yeast, salt, anise seed and sugar. He beat in the liquids and eggs. Finally, he kneaded all of his ingredients together until they turned smooth and it pulled back like taffy. "Cut this orange," he said to Felix.

It dawned on me that Felix had somehow morphed into the son my dad never had and the other way around. I smiled. I didn't mind sharing my dad if it kept Felix around.

We waited for the masa to rise. "I like to let it sit and rest longer usually, but an hour should be enough," my dad said. He showed Felix how to punch it down and shape it into small loaves that resembled skulls and traditional rounds. They stuck the loaves in the oven and chatted about Felix's school. After a while, my dad pulled out the tray and glazed the loaves with the juice of the orange Felix had cut.

"The finishing touch," I said. I pulled out the necessary supplies and showed Felix how to decorate the loaves with candied fruit and colored sugar. My stomach was in revolution mode. I faked a cough, hoping to drown out any unwelcomed sounds.

"It looks great," Felix said.

"Try it." My dad motioned to the tray.

Felix tore off a piece and shoved it into his mouth. His jaw slowly worked up and down, side to side. His eyebrows shot up. He took a deep breath through his nose. His jaw relaxed. "Absolutely delicious!"

We polished off half the tray.

"Now all you need is the altar," Felix said.

"We've never had one of those."

"But there's always a first time," I said to my dad. Never mind that Día de los Muertos was months away. "We've got lots of stuff in the basement."

I climbed down to the basement and looked for my mom's big red wooden heirloom box. It sat on one of the high shelves. I set up the ladder to pull it down. I pulled and pushed the heavy cargo up the stairs.

Felix came to the doorway. "Let me help," he said. He scooped it up as if it weighed no more than a cookie. I halfway wished there was more stuff, just to watch him do that again.

Felix set the box down in the middle of the front room. I grabbed a plastic spatula and pried it open. My abuelita Carmelita's lace tablecloths sat below some of my mom's other things, wrapped in tissue paper. I brought one up to my nose. It still smelled of incense and Vicks VapoRub. I rummaged through the rest of the things. There was a small Virgin of Guadalupe and baby Jesus made of painted wood.

I caught Felix staring at me from the other side of the box. I couldn't help hoping it meant he thought about me in the same way I thought about him. "How should we set this up?" he asked.

"I don't know. Like the ones in church."

We pulled out several items: the tablecloth, the Virgin, and Jesus. We put everything else back in and closed the box. I covered it with the folded tablecloth to use as the base of the altar.

"It's missing something," I said. I walked into the kitchen and grabbed the picture of abuelita Carmelita. It was one of the few pictures that hung on our walls. The picture was old. It had faded. It was a good picture otherwise. Her hair hadn't grayed, and her face was smooth and young.

I laid the photo on the tablecloth of our altar. I draped purple ribbons on it to fill the white space.

"It's too low," my dad said from his seat at the counter.

"Where else are we going to put it?" I shrugged.

"Drag it to the window for the passersby to see." He walked over and removed an empty rack from the window. Felix grabbed a couple of cinder blocks from the gangway. He put them on the floor, in the space my dad had just cleared. They moved to the center of the room and carefully lifted up the box. They set it down on top of the cinder blocks without unsettling a single ribbon. My dad took a couple of loaves of Day of the Dead bread and placed them on a plate on the altar. They sat in perfect eye's view. He disappeared and returned with a white candle in a clear glass. He lit it and added it to the altar. "Father Arturo gave it to me a while back," he said.

"What time is it?" Felix asked.

"Five."

"I should go. Belinda thinks I haven't been spending enough time with the other businesses."

"Go. We don't want to get you in trouble," my dad said. He was speaking for himself, because I didn't care what Belinda thought.

"I can't help it if I like hanging out here." Felix winked. He was almost flirting.

I smiled. "I'll walk you out," I said.

Felix and I stood on the sidewalk in front of Burciaga's. Neither of us spoke. He rummaged through his backpack as if he was the nervous one this time. "So," he said. "I'm supposed to drop off some business books at Wong's Taco Shop. Do you want to come with me?"

"Sure."

"*La Gran Pirámide* looks incredible."

"Yes, and it's going to look more incredible each day now that Colonel Franco agreed to let everyone—not just the boys—help outside with the construction."

"Maybe I can come tomorrow morning to help too. It's funny how you guys call him Colonel Franco."

"Well, he is a colonel."

"He's in the Army?"

"Retired."

"I didn't know that."

"There's nothing to know. After Colonel Franco retired from the Army and his wife died, he got really really bored. Iker says that's why his grandpa volunteers for everything. Last year, he directed our school play after they laid off the first round of teachers at American Academy."

"Sounds hysterical. I mean Colonel Franco as a drama director, not your teachers losing their jobs. See, it's true that I really don't know anyone else here that well. You and your dad are the only ones I really talk to. I visit with the others, but it's not like this."

More time with the others meant less time with us. I changed the subject. "What were you and my dad making yesterday anyway?"

"Agave molasses."

"Agave? I've read about that. That's the stuff they make tequila out of, right?"

"Yes. We're using the nectar. Agave nectar is a sweetener pressed from the plant, like tapping maple syrup. It's supposed to be healthier than sugar."

"It was like gum. I had to run it under hot water for a long time so I could scrape it off the pans."

"That's because of what we did to it to try and make it into molasses. I'm sorry. I should've soaked the pans. My mother taught me better than that."

"Do you miss your mom?"

"I do. But she's also the reason I'm here. I want to do my part."

I missed my mom too, but I didn't say so. I didn't want our afternoon turning into a pity party. "My dad really likes you," I said instead.

"Do you like me?" he asked. The heat rose to my cheeks. I looked at my foot.

I looked up again. We were somehow now in the alley behind one of the abandoned buildings south of the bakery. I backed up against the wall. Felix's face hovered two inches from mine. I breathed in his smokiness. He reached over my head and braced himself on the wall.

That thing fluttered inside me.

This could be it, I thought. I shut my eyes and raised my face up to his. His lips crashed down on mine. It wasn't like I'd imagined. No, his lips were rough. I stepped back. Maybe Felix could read my mind. His savage lips went Dr. Jekyl. They parted against mine, soft and gentle. He tasted of fruit sprinkled with salt. I wanted the earth to open up and swallow us whole. I wanted to die in the moment.

He pulled away. "That was nice," he said.

I opened my eyes, and we were back on the sidewalk. It happened so fast, I wasn't sure it'd happened at all. He walked down the street. I stumbled behind him. The fluttering didn't stop. That thing inside me kicked up the air. "I like you," I mumbled.

He stopped at Wong's doorstep. "Time to go in. See you soon?" I nodded. He squeezed my hand and disappeared into Wong's Taco Shop

I kept thinking about Felix's playdough lips, textured with fingerprints, soft as if molded, soft like warm rolls, soft to kiss. I thought I might fly away. I didn't walk. I floated home.

A song lived inside me. *Felix, Felix.*

I anchored myself to the front steps of the bakery and closed my eyes. I put my palm on my chest. I'd waited my whole life to fall in love. I didn't believe I exactly had to be loved back in order to call it falling in love, and I was sure that this is what I was feeling. Never mind that I still didn't understand what his connection to Belinda was. Never mind that there were bigger things to worry about than boys.

I opened my eyes and looked out at the valley of empty buildings. The beacon of steel, brick and mortar jutted out above everything on the southeast side of Pig Park. I sat out there until the night shadows nudged me to go inside. I went to my room, flung myself on my bed, and listened to the possibilities.

CHAPTER 31

The oven clunked and moaned—on the verge of swallowing my dad. He crouched halfway inside its iron jaws. "Is that safe?" I asked.

"They don't make them like they used to. When I was an apprentice baker, we used a coal oven."

"That was a long time ago."

No oven meant no morning bread and nothing to clean up.

I walked to the Nowak's.

Mrs. Nowak had a green thumb. She grew most of the vegetables for the grocery store herself in the summer. There were herbs in the basement, corn on the rooftop and everything else in the backyard. The day was so hot that half the vegetable bushes Mrs. Nowak had planted in the backyard had thrown up their arms and turned over in the heat.

Marcos and Josefina walked out the door. "Your tomatoes are dying." I pointed at the sideways bushes.

"Nah, my mom just sprinkles them with water at night, and they bounce right back." Marcos smiled.

Maybe the pyramid was like water to Pig Park.

I looked at Josefina and waited to see if she noticed anything different about me. My dad had acted normal enough in the morning. I'd spent half the night looking in the mirror.

I waited the whole walk to the park, but Josefina didn't say anything. It was just as well. I didn't want to talk about Felix in front of Marcos. I didn't feel like getting teased. More importantly, he didn't need to know.

We walked up to the pyramid and went inside. Felix was there. He flashed his white teeth. The smile wasn't any different than usual, but the heat still rose to my face. I put my hands over my cheeks until I could look at him again.

Maybe I had imagined the kiss.

I looked around the room. A jumble of wires and pipes had somehow made it onto the walls. Colonel Franco cleared his throat. "A contractor friend of Jorge Peregrino's came in during the weekend and laid out the electrical and plumbing. He pulled in lines from the street lamps and the park's sprinkler system. All we have to do is tack on the walls."

Mr. Nowak pulled up in Peregrino's van and parallel-parked ten feet away. Blonde plywood sat stacked high on the luggage racks. The back doors were tied closed to make room for even more wood. The weight of the load pushed the white steel frame of the van low on its tires so that the exhaust almost scrapped the street.

"I went out looking for drywall. I got a much better deal on these wood panels. They won't require taping or paint," he explained. He tapped the side of the van with his large hand. The boys erupted into applause.

"Good thinking, Dad." Marcos patted Mr. Nowak on the back.

"Less work for us," Pedro Wong said.

"I'll leave the keys here. You can get the van back to Peregrino when you're done." Mr. Nowak tossed the keys at Colonel Franco and waved good-bye.

"Pair up and start unloading," Colonel Franco said to us. "Stack them flat, and put a couple of four by fours between each. We need to acclimate the wood before we can use it."

Each panel was only about an inch thick, but they were tall and wide enough to keep us from moving more than a stack of two or three at a time. It was so hot that I could feel the salt oozing from my pores. I was grateful to have on a tank top.

Claudia Guadalupe Martínez   171

Most of the boys stripped off their shirts, but Felix was modest. He kept on his yellow polo shirt.

"Rain would be nice," Josefina said. "We haven't had a good rainfall since May."

"Yes, rain would be nice," I said. I didn't even care that the rain around here had the habit of wetting the muck the company had left behind in the soil, making our entire neighborhood smell like chicharrones. I could live with the smell of pork rinds if it meant cooling off.

Colonel Franco left and returned with a couple of cans and paintbrushes. "Brush the inside brick with this to help repel moisture," he said. "It will prevent molding once we place the panels."

We stroked the bare sections of wall with our paintbrushes.

Felix was gone by lunchtime. I didn't pay attention to much of anything the rest of the afternoon. I didn't even ogle Marcos in his skin suit. I just wanted to hurry up and get back to the bakery in case Felix decided to pay us a visit.

I walked home as soon as Colonel Franco said we were done for the day. I found Felix deep in conversation with my dad. Felix's hair was a mess. His cheek and yellow shirt were streaked with soot. That and the empty display cases meant the oven was still out.

"I couldn't tell anything from just climbing in," he said.

"We could pay to have someone come out and take a closer look, but they don't make these anymore. They'll have a hard time finding parts. Even with new parts, it'll just be a bandaid. The only real solution is to buy a new one."

"It's a big investment."

"With the money that *La Gran Pirámide* will bring, it won't matter. Let me run upstairs and grab that catalog I got in the mail," he said and disappeared.

I pointed at Felix's cheek. "You got something there." I didn't want to talk about the oven, I wanted to talk about what had happened in the alley.

My dad returned with an armful of catalogs. "I can bake upstairs for a while. But a new oven is an investment."

Felix and my dad flipped through the catalogs together. They compared prices on the Internet until it got dark and Felix went home. I waited for my dad to fall asleep, planning to pull out my bike and follow Felix. I wanted to know if the kiss had been real.

I must've been tired from actually getting to work outside because I fell asleep first.

CHAPTER 32

Colonel Franco told us exactly what to do and showed us how to do each task. The boys framed the inside walls of the pyramid using four-by-fours. They trimmed the first panel to height and propped it up using a level. Marcos covered a hammer with a rag to protect the finish on the panel and pounded the nails every four to six inches along the edge of the wood frame. He moved from one edge to the other.

They repeated this with each panel.

"Be sure to leave a few millimeters in between each panel to avoid expansion problems," Colonel Franco said. "The panels will expand with the humidity."

Josefina and I measured the electrical switches and plumbing and sketched the measurements onto the panels. Felix took a small jigsaw and cut out the marked sections.

"I have to leave early again to help Belinda. I won't be able to come to the bakery after," Felix said. He cut the last panel and headed out.

I couldn't help feeling shortchanged. Marcos stared after him. "He's not one of us, Masi."

I looked at Marcos. What did it matter that Felix hadn't grown up in Pig Park? Maybe that wasn't what Marcos was getting at, so I replied with the only other thing I could think of. "Jealousy doesn't suit you, Marcos." Marcos shrugged and stomped away. Felix was making it so that Marcos finally saw me as more than a kid sister type. Was that it? Probably not, but it didn't matter. I liked Felix.

Once all the panels were in place, we nailed on the plastic molding. "It's getting late. Let's wrap things up," Colonel Franco said. "I will see you tomorrow."

I walked home and found Loretta standing outside the bakery. I held the door open and she squeezed through. "What can I get for you, Loretta?"

"I came to see if you guys had fixed the oven."

"We haven't. My dad cranked out a batch of ginger pigs and baguette rolls in the kitchen upstairs this morning."

"That's very resourceful." She proceeded with a half-hour exposition on the state of affairs in the neighborhood. She gave her opinion on everything from the inside of the pyramid to the paleta vendor who had set up at the park when the construction started. She'd seen him picking his nose when he thought no one was looking.

She paced back and forth in front of the door. She opened her mouth and closed it. She looked me up and down. "I've been worried about your dad," she finally said.

"He's fine."

"Really?"

"Fine."

"Mija, but how does he feel?"

"What do you mean?"

"She left him."

"Oh," I said. She always knew more than anyone gave her credit for, but she didn't seem to know that my dad was set on a reconciliation. Of course, it was none of her business as usual. I wanted to tell her so. She was making me uncomfortable. "My mom will be back," I said instead, even though I didn't exactly believe it yet.

The answer satisfied her, because she didn't push. "Mija," she said, "they've been tearing up one of those old American Lard housing buildings over by the train stop. I saw that Belinda girl out there. She up and bought the building."

"I didn't hear anything about that." Felix hadn't mentioned that the real estate thing was for real.

"I bet you Jorge Peregrino knows something. I'll see you later, and I'll keep you and your dad posted."

"Enjoy your night, Loretta."

"You too, Masi." She strolled down the street toward the flower shop.

I stuck my neck into the stairwell and called up to the living room. "Dad? Are you still up there?"

"I'm working on recipes," he yelled.

I locked up, washed the dishes and put everything away.

CHAPTER 33

I couldn't stop thinking about what Loretta had said. None of the Sanchezes knew how to leave well enough alone. I pulled out the bike and headed down the street toward the building Loretta had mentioned.

A large dumpster had appeared in the middle of the street. The building's insides hung all around it like the wires of a broken appliance. There were discarded walls and pipes everywhere. It was late and hard to imagine what was going on. The building had taped on curtains, fashioned from newspaper, covering the work from people like Loretta and me.

Low voices streamed from the back of the building. There was laughter, Belinda's loopy laughter. I slipped down the side of the building. A swirl of smoke drifted up into the sky. It smelled of burning tires and angry skunk.

I'm not sure why I didn't announce myself. Maybe I figured that if Felix had wanted me around, he would've invited me. I put my face up to the slats of the wooden fence and just listened and watched. Belinda sat on a lawn chair with an old man's pipe in her hand. Felix sat on a plastic milk crate nearby.

"You're a good guy, Felix," she said. She puffed on her pipe. She patted Felix on the head like a dog. He shrugged her off. "You're a good boy."

"This is what you've been up to the whole time? Why you would go along with this?" His voice was harsh.

"You and I define success in different ways. Even father defines success differently. This is a job, Felix. You do these people a disservice to think otherwise." She pushed her pipe at him. He pushed it away. His lips curled like he'd just bit into a piece of moldy bread.

"You're heartless. This isn't right," he said.

"Feelings don't matter in the end."

"I don't believe that."

"That's because you're good. Didn't I just say that?"

"You don't have to be good to believe in something. Maybe believing in something can make you good."

"You're not listening to me. More and more as of late." Or maybe he just didn't understand what she was talking about, like me.

"You mean less and less. That's because I can't listen to this anymore. I'm out." He stood, his back to me. He leaned down into her. He was going to kiss her. I was sure of it. I squeezed my eyes shut. I couldn't bear to watch. I stopped breathing. Nothing else mattered. That thing inside my chest kicked at my ribs.

I stepped back and tripped on a bottle. It rolled down the sidewalk and into the gutter. I ran.

"Who's there?" Felix called out. "Who is that? Hey, wait!"

I jumped on my bike and peddled hard. Tears boiled to the surface and streamed down my cheeks. Halfway down the block, I looked over my shoulder. Felix stopped to catch his breath. He yelled something at me that I couldn't hear and threw his hands up in the air.

I pushed my feet down even harder until I made it home.

I wiped my face with the collar of my T-shirt. I could barely see straight. I closed my eyes and shook my head. I took a deep breath and opened the door. I sniffled into the inside of my elbow and tried to look like it was just another night in Pig Park.

My dad sat at the kitchen table, scribbling into his note cards. He hummed a romantico song under his breath.

"Looking at recipes again?" I asked in a tiny little voice.

"Something like that," he said. He held up the card. There were five lines in Spanish.

"Is it a poem?"

"Could be. Good food is lyrical like poetry," he said.

"Takes the perfect blend of flavors, textures and aromas. Don't look at me like that. I work with my hands, but that doesn't mean I don't know things."

"I didn't say that. Has my mom called?"

"Yes. I told her to call back later."

"You talked to her?"

"Yes. We talked for awhile."

"Hmm." I waited, but he didn't volunteer any other information. I forced a smile. I walked upstairs and barricaded myself in my room to cry some more.

CHAPTER 34

My dad set down a tray of ginger pigs and a tray of bolillos in a series of swift movements. He was a regular bread ninja. "It's a beautiful morning," he said.

I grumbled.

Somewhere deep inside I was happy for him that he and my mom had talked. Maybe she was finally coming back. But I couldn't share in it. There was all kinds of other junk rattling around in my head.

"I'm staying home today," I said. I wanted to crawl back into bed.

"If that's how you want to treat your responsibilities."

"I guess not." I couldn't help feeling guilty and selfish.

I was the last one to arrive at the park.

"Listen up, everyone. We are done with the construction," Colonel Franco said. Everyone applauded. They patted each other on the back.

"That was fast," Josefina said.

"Yep. Like Colonel Franco said: two triangles here,

two triangles there." A pyramid was little more than simple geometry. Plus, Peregrino's friends had done the hard parts. I know I should've been a little sad that we were done. Our summer together was almost over. I wasn't sad though—for once. I wanted to get away from Felix, and I wanted to go home.

I started walking away.

"Not so fast," Colonel Franco said. "You got one more thing to do. We're decorating today. Then, you can go home. Felix, did you bring the boxes Belinda gave you?"

"I need help getting them here."

"Pick a volunteer." Colonel Franco motioned at us with his hand.

"Masi," Felix said. I shrunk back. I opened my mouth to protest, but nothing came out. I looked over to Josefina a few feet away. She shrugged.

"I'll go," Marcos said.

"No," Felix said.

"Stop messing around and someone just go." Colonel Franco interrupted.

"Masi," Felix repeated. Felix didn't waste any more time. He put his hand on my back and steered me toward the sidewalk. I stumbled along.

"Masi, I don't know what you heard last night," he said.

"I didn't really hear anything, but I saw," I said. My breath caught inside my throat.

"What did you see?"

"You kissed her." The words were sawdust in my mouth.

"Belinda?"

"Yes. You kissed Belinda, after you kissed me." Felix chuckled. My hands balled into fists.

"I didn't kiss her. Not like that. Belinda is my sister."

"What? She doesn't even look like you."

"She's my half-sister. My mother was once a student of Dr. Vidales Casal. It was before he was a big deal. She didn't know he was married or that he had a family. When I came along, he acted like he didn't even know her name. She dropped out of college to get a job because of me."

"Dr. Vidales Casal is your dad?" That thing inside me twitched.

"He doesn't publicly acknowledge it. That's why I use my mom's last name. Belinda uses her mom's last name too: Fitzgerald. She's not perfect, but at least she accepts me as her brother. She helped me get my scholarship and got me here. It's important for me to finish school fast so maybe I can help my mom finish her degree too. My mom shouldn't have to be a waitress forever because of me."

"Wow."

"Yes, wow. Belinda has a big mouth sometimes, but I don't tell people. I told you because I don't want you to get the wrong idea about me. I care about what you and your dad think. You've been good to me."

"I won't tell anyone else," I said. It dawned on me that even with my mom gone, it could be worse.

We walked into the warehouse. "Belinda is out. Jorge is in the back doing inventory," he said. His eyes locked in on me. "Now that you're not mad at me, can I ask you for something? Can you help me talk your dad out of buying that oven when I come by this afternoon."

"Ok." I didn't know why Felix would even care about my dad buying that oven, but I agreed. Jumping to conclusions hadn't done me any good the night before.

Felix stacked four boxes on one dolly and three on another. He passed me the handles of the dolly with less boxes and grabbed the other one. He hummed as we pushed the boxes back to the park.

I walked over to Josefina's side. She nudged me with her elbow.

"Everything okay?"

I nodded.

"Come on, what are you waiting for?" Colonel Franco asked. The ladder was already propped up against the wall.

We each took a few items. There was a variety of colorful clay suns and moons. We hung them along each of the four walls. We placed a statue of La Muerte at the center and arranged an army of skeleton dolls in action clusters—macabre renditions of the department store window scenes they put up downtown every Christmas. We lined the outer edges of the pyramid's floor with hundreds of candles. The last candle fell into place just before midday, and everyone cheered. We were finally finished.

"I have to return the dollies, but I'll be by in a little while," Felix said to me.

Josefina and I walked home together. I couldn't hold it anymore. I told her about the kiss. I told her almost everything, but left out the business about Belinda. I had promised Felix not to tell anyone about his family secret. The words jumbled in my mouth trying to explain what I felt.

"Why were you so out of it this morning then? Is your mom okay?"

"She's okay. I guess I was just feeling weird about the whole Felix thing."

"Because of Belinda?"

"No," I said.

"Be careful. Felix is like a drug. You should hear yourself," she said.

I laughed. Maybe none of it made sense. That was okay. I knew what I wanted, and Belinda wasn't standing in my way.

CHAPTER 35

My dad pushed a tray of ginger pigs in front of my face. I breathed in their warm spice. "Eat one," he said. I tore at the auburn flesh and put the piece of perfect plump pig in my mouth. The flaky top gave way against my teeth. Its buttery tissue melted on my tongue. "How is it?" he asked.

"As delicious as ever. I could eat these for breakfast, lunch and dinner."

"We did it." Felix smiled. I didn't know what he was talking about, but I smiled back.

"Those aren't regular *marranitos*." My dad pulled an index card out of his pocket and pushed it at me. It was a folded card like the one I'd taken for a love poem. "Look at the ingredients."

I squinted and made out the Spanish word for flour. *Harina.* "Huh?"

"No sugar in these," he continued. He snatched the card back. "I made them for your mother, so she can have sweet bread even with her diabetes."

"Dad, she's going to love these." I threw my arms around him. "You're a genius."

Felix grabbed a ginger pig. Greasy outlines on the tray, like the body outlines at a crime scene, revealed that it wasn't his first.

"What's in them anyway?" I asked.

"Felix told me about all these natural products I could substitute for our homemade molasses and other ingredients. We experimented."

"First we tried Stevia. It's a ground up sweetleaf from South America. But there was an aftertaste. It couldn't produce the right color for the bread either. There was also Agave syrup, from the agave plants. We just couldn't get it to the right consistency. Finally, we got on the Internet and discovered Yacón syrup. It's native to Peru and comes from the roots of the yacón plant. It's made with an evaporator, the same way as maple syrup and the taste is closer to molasses," Felix said.

"I tweaked my recipe for *marranitos* around the substitutes. I also adjusted the amount of baking soda, and there you have it."

"I think you can sell these."

"I really made them for my wife. With the cost of Yacón syrup it would be hard to break even. Hold on,

Felix. Let me grab the stuff to show Masi." My dad disappeared into the kitchen.

Felix grabbed my wrist, taking me by surprise. His fingers were warm and moist. "Don't forget what we talked about," he said.

"What?" His touch was making it so that I couldn't think straight.

"Back in the warehouse. You said you would help me stop your dad from buying a new oven. We're talking about a couple thousand dollars even for a used one." He dropped my hand.

I held my wrist. "Don't worry. We don't even have any money. He can't buy anything without money." We were late on all the bills and all of our savings were gone.

My dad returned and handed me the bottle of Yacón syrup. I looked at the label.

"Yacón is cheaper if you buy it in bulk, I'm sure," Felix said. "You can special price the new recipe. And, you can save up the money for the syrup if you don't buy that oven. I did a little research. There's a place in Indiana that rents kitchen equipment."

"No, Felix. I already ordered the new oven," my dad said.

It was the first I'd heard of it. "You have? Can you cancel it?" I asked.

"It's done."

"How did you even pay for it?"

"I took out a line of credit."

My mouth dropped open. No one in his or her right mind would give him credit. Not with those notices from the bank sitting in that drawer. I took it to mean he'd borrowed money from my grandparents. How had he managed that? He'd just started talking to my mom again. Asking my grandparents to dip into their saving was something he'd never ever done before.

"I'm happy with my decision. Felix, I hope you'll help me set it up when it arrives," he said. His face hardened. I didn't see that look too much, and it told me to leave it alone.

Felix nodded and excused himself, looking both displeased and resigned. I cleaned up as soon as it was time to close and followed my dad upstairs.

"Have you told Mom about these?" I asked.

"Not yet. I'm thinking I'd rather have her taste them."

"Are we mailing her a care package?"

"Or maybe she's coming back."

"You won her back?" I jumped.

"It's too soon to tell. Let's make another batch of Patricia's *marranitos*."

"Sure. But you can't call them that. It's not very romantic to have someone attach the word pig to your name. The name should describe the thing. If I had to name them, I would name these 'Skinny Pigs.'"

"I like the sound of that. Skinny Pigs."

He pulled out everything we needed. I put on a pot of coffee. I watched him stir together shortening, baking soda, cinnamon and vanilla until the mixture formed a firm paste. He beat in the yacón syrup, eggs and milk. He gradually added flour to form the masa. Since it was more cake or cookie than it was actual bread, we didn't have to wait for the dough to rise. He rolled out the masa and cut it with the pig-shaped cookie cutters. Finally, he brushed them with egg wash, and popped them into the oven.

The phone rang. He dove for it, not letting it get to a second ring.

"Patricia," he said. "We were just making something...We have something delicious for you...It's sweet...Not as sweet as you. No, you'll have to come get it..."

He was worse than those guys in the cheesy soap operas. I was sure I'd end up with diabetes too if I listened any longer. I groaned, but fought back a smile. He missed her.

I was happy for him. Maybe, just maybe, I was also growing less mad at her.

CHAPTER 36

The roar of an engine announced Belinda's arrival. Her shiny black SUV tankered onto the lawn and parked parallel to the pyramid.

Those standing scrambled to find seats.

Loretta Sanchez stuck her head inside the pyramid before taking a seat on the mismatch of chairs set up just outside its door. Casey and Stacey plopped down on the thirsty afternoon grass on either side of Marcos. Casey played with his hair. They whispered things into each of his ears. I didn't care. I looked away.

"You kids did a wonderful job," my dad said.

"It could use some windows," Loretta said.

"Don't pay any attention to her, kids. Whoever heard of a pyramid with windows?"

Felix popped out from the passenger's side of the SUV and sat next to Josefina and me. Belinda adjusted the rearview mirror, fixed the collar of her shirt, and climbed out.

Colonel Franco struggled to his feet and stood beside Belinda. "Ok, now that everyone is here, I'm going to make this quick," he said. "I know you are all excited about the big unveil just a few days away and you should be. This will be a very short meeting so we can all get back to our preparations. As a final order of business, I'd like to motion for us to relocate the Pig Park Chamber of Commerce here to *La Gran Pirámide*."

"I second the motion," my dad said. There wasn't much arguing this time. A series of 'ayes' followed, making it a unanimous decision.

"See, I told you it'd be quick. Belinda has something she'd like to talk to the kids about now. As per an earlier conversation, I think they can handle this on their own. Please excuse me." Colonel Franco slowly made his way home, and the other grown-ups followed suit. Felix jumped up from his seat.

"What's going on, Felix?" I asked.

"This is all Belinda. I'm going back to the warehouse. I'll see you later." He walked away shaking his head. I frowned. I didn't understand.

Belinda waited until all eyes were on her. "Ok. I have something for you," she said. She stood up and flipped open the back door of her SUV. She had converted the cargo compartment into a makeshift closet. Two aluminum racks sagged at the center from the weight of their contents. Belinda squatted on the back bumper. We crowded around for a closer look.

"What is that?" I asked.

"It's a gift. This is the finishing touch. Masi, you suggested nice shirts. Felix was really into the idea, so I suggested you take it one step further and dress the part. Peasant shirts, guayaveras, sombreros, mariachi hats," she said.

My mouth dropped open.

She handed me a fuchsia peasant shirt embroidered with wild flowers, and Josefina a lime green one. Casey and Stacey received a pair of red flamenco style shirts. They held the ruffled confections against their torsos and twirled around. The guys received guayaberas. And there were still enough outfits to spare.

"It's like the wardrobe trailer for a mariachi movie," Josefina said.

"It's all very cha-cha," Marcos snickered. He waved the peach short-sleeved dress shirt with lace columns down the front, still on the hanger. "I'm not wearing this. These are the kind of shirts old men wear to baptisms and first communions. No one is going to take a guy named Nowak seriously wearing this."

"If they can make American Lard in a foreign

country, and a guy named Wong can sell tacos and chicharrones, then you can wear this. It's called globalization," Belinda said.

"I'm a Chino-Latino. Get your story straight," Pedro Wong complained.

"Globo-li-what? Is that something to do with balloons? Globos?" Casey asked.

"It's exploitation. That's what it is," Marcos went on.

"If people can exploit the American flag on Memorial day and the Fourth of July, then you can exploit anything. It's fair in a free market economy," Belinda argued.

"How come our parents don't have to wear this frilly stuff?" Iker wanted to know.

"We're the free labor and the face," Pedro nodded at Marcos.

"Frilly isn't the word. This is just plain dumb. We're not cheap puppets you can dress up. We are not caricatures." Marcos threw his shirt back into the back of the SUV. He had a point.

"Your product could be the best in the world. If your image doesn't draw people to you, no one will ever know it. These authentic, quality garments celebrate what you're doing here."

I looked closely at the stitching in my hands. I turned it inside out. There was no special tag. But they were still costumes. They were no different than anything that ever graced the stage at one of American Academy's school plays. The clothes were Belinda's outsider idea of what we were.

"These aren't costumes." Belinda objected as if reading my mind. "They came all the way from Jalisco and Tamaulipas. You are very lucky Dr. Vidales Casal happened to be traveling through the interior."

"Interior of what?" Josefina asked.

"Ugh, abroad. These clothes have a purpose. There are restaurants, bakeries, and flower shops all across the city. Something has to make people choose Pig Park."

"That's what the pyramid is for," I interrupted.

"Yes, you built *La Gran Pirámide*. I'm talking about creating an entire experience to go with it." Belinda laughed her loopy laugh. "These clothes commit you to the experience. You have to calculate and capitalize on all of your assets."

"You mean like the flowers?" Stacey asked.

"No, I mean you go all the way. You start with the clothes, then you speak the part. Flavor your words. Give them some Spanish, but not so much that you scare them away. This is *Parque Puerco* from here on out."

"No offense," I said to Belinda. "*Parque Puerco* translates to Pork Park. We're Pig Park."

"And no one will know the difference when this place disappears off the map. I thought you wanted to save this place."

"We do. Like Colonel Franco always says, we can't give up now," Freddy Fernandez said. Frank Fernandez nodded his head.

I wanted to tell them to stop agreeing and nodding. I wanted to stand up and tell Belinda that she was nuts. I sat there and thought long and hard before opening my mouth again. Belinda was Felix's sister. We had already gotten off to a bad start. I needed to try harder. We were desperate. Besides, no one had ever died from wearing a shirt. I took the shirt, put it on over my clothes, and walked home.

CHAPTER 37

Felix's voice carried up from the sidewalk. I jumped out of bed and found Felix talking to my dad downstairs. "You're here early, Felix," my dad said.

"There isn't much else left for me to do."

"You should do something fun then, go downtown or something. Summer is almost over. Before you know it, you'll be an old man like me who's done nothing but work. We won't tell on you."

I sprouted valor like wings. "My dad's right. I'll go with you downtown so you don't get lost, if you want."

"Ok." Felix shrugged.

I grabbed my backpack and dumped out all the crumpled-up homework from the previous year. I threw in a water bottle, a hoodie, gum and all of my savings—which added up to nineteen dollars. I was ready to run away.

We walked to the train stop. "I thought about asking Belinda to see if she wanted to come, but she's got her hands full," he said.

"What's she doing?"

Felix hesitated. "Fixing up that old building."

I smiled. Maybe it meant Felix would stay past the summer. "Did she really buy a building?"

Felix hesitated again. "No. The Old Goat—Dr. Vidales Casal—paid for it. It's his building."

"He's moving here?" I asked.

"No." This time his answer was quick. While I didn't understand what the doctor wanted with it then, it had to be better than letting the birds and cobwebs swallow it up. I knew Dr. Vidales Casal was Felix's sore spot, so I didn't push.

Felix inserted a couple of dollars into an automated machine, and retrieved a train card. He slid it once for each of us, and we pushed through the turnstile. We were the only two humans on the platform. A squirrel looked at us out of the corner of its beady eye and gnawed at something between two doll-sized hands.

We took seats near the entrance of the train. I looked out the window at the city flying by. Several stretches of road looked devastated to the point of desertion. There were a few enclaves of clean new neighborhoods throbbing with life. They looked like small suburbs with tall buildings.

We exited at the first stop downtown.

Large neon signs advertised delicious things to eat. Hot dogs. Noodles. Deep dish pizza. Iridescent road signs pointed to daily parking that cost more than the bakery made in a week. There were school buses and charter buses parked along the streets with their hazard lights blinking red and angry. They unloaded school children, parents, senior citizens, people who looked like they had someplace to go, people who looked lost.

Languages I didn't speak buzzed all around. Cameras snapped away down the street. An old man scrolled a device, then stuck it back in his fanny pack. A young couple argued over something on a piece of paper. Businessmen and women pushed through the hordes alongside us on their way to work.

"Look at all these people. We should've brought some flyers to pass around for *La Gran Pirámide's* unveiling," Felix pointed out. "I don't know where to start. What should we do, Masi?"

"My mom likes coming downtown to see the Christmas windows. But it's not Christmas."

"No, it's not Christmas."

"You know that old movie about the kid who takes the day off from school?"

"He crashes that parade, sneaks into the fancy restaurant, and visits the art museum."

"Yes, the Art Institute. They shot that movie here."

I sprinted down the street. Felix paused, then ran up behind me and jumped on the back of one of the bronze lions that guarded the museum gates. I climbed the mountain of stairs two at a time. Felix hopped off the lion and motioned for me to follow. We walked through the doors at the tail end of a large tour group, unnoticed by the ushers.

We followed the crowd into one of the rooms. A half-painted canvas filled the wall. The stuff in the adjoining room was straight out of a pirate ship or a castle. "The pyramid isn't like this at all," I said.

"Well, it shouldn't be." Felix looked like he was thinking. "It should be its own self, just how Pig Park is its own self. Never mind what Belinda says." The corners of my mouth pushed against my cheeks. I smiled. I kept the bit about the shirts and mariachi hats to myself. I wanted to just enjoy my day with Felix.

We moved quietly through the exhibits and walked out just as we'd walked in. I was undone by the sunlight. I squinted and covered my eyes with my hands. "There are stores all along that street." I pointed north of the museum and walked in that direction.

Felix pushed through the glass door of the shop on the corner. The cashier glared at us from the corner of her eye like we were a pair of rats climbing out of the sewer. "I don't like this place," he said and walked out.

He sauntered toward a street vendor. A lady with waist-length hair extensions stood before an array of knickknacks on the sidewalk. She smiled at us. Felix handed her three dollars and took a keychain with an imprint of the Chicago skyline. "I haven't bought anything for my mom," he said.

"It's hot. Want to go over by the fountain?" I asked.

"Sure."

The fountain was big enough to swim laps in. Water shot twenty feet in the air. A group in Maple Leafs T-shirts took advantage of the light and snapped a series of goofy pictures. Felix and I moved along the edge to the shady side.

"Anything else you want to do?" I asked. I fiddled with my hair.

"I don't know. What do you want to do?"

"I don't know."

Felix looked at me. He leaned. The thing inside me fluttered, and I braced myself. I closed my eyes. His soft lips landed on mine. I reached for his face. A southbound breeze slapped the fountain water so that it sprayed down all around us. It was a kiss in the rain that ended before that thing inside me really kicked up the dust. I opened my eyes. Droplets of water evaporated off Felix's skin and steamed.

"That shouldn't have happened again. It was an impulse. I'm sorry," he said.

"It was nice."

"I shouldn't have done it again."

"Why?" I didn't understand. We weren't making bombs or selling drugs to third-graders. Maybe I'd read things wrong. Maybe I had bad breath or he simply didn't like me like that after all.

"We should go." Felix pushed through the crowds. I struggled to keep up.

The landscape of the city flew past the windows of the train. His mouth was a vault locked shut. We were back in Pig Park and on our separate ways in the blink of an eye.

I walked home alone, with my thoughts still wrapped around that kiss. I wanted to kick myself. I didn't understand. Felix could make me feel so good one minute, and terrible the next. What was his problem? I grew mad. I was mad at myself for getting caught up in something as simple as a kiss.

CHAPTER 38

My dad and I watched the freight truck squeeze onto our street and stop in front of the bakery. Two red-faced men, an overweight one and a skinny one, hopped out.

"Delivery for Burciaga," the overweight one said.

"Yes, right in here." My dad propped the door open.

The overweight man returned to his truck and rolled open the back, revealing several rows of large commercial kitchen appliances. His skinny companion pushed one of the metallic monsters to the edge. He hit a protruding red button that lowered the rear end of the truck like an elevator. They strapped it to a dolly and huffed and puffed their way up the stoop.

"Right back here." My dad led them to kitchen. "I pulled the old oven out so you won't have trouble."

"Do you want us to dispose of that?" the overweight one asked. He pointed to our old clunker sitting in the corner, up against the display cases.

"No need. Thank you so much. I've made other arrangements."

Since the street was too narrow for the eighteen-wheeler to turn around, the two men inched out in reverse.

Marcos and the Fernandez brothers helped Felix haul the old clunker away later that afternoon. Money issues aside, I was relieved to see it go—to be rid of its mood swings. The thing was as moody as Felix.

I shadowed the boys as they rolled the old oven down the street on a pair of skateboards. They lifted it and pushed it into the industrial dumpster outside Belinda's building. Felix had called my dad and informed him that the dumpster, which lay kitty corner from the park, was paid for. It would save us the disposal fee.

Marcos and the Fernandez brothers went one way. I followed Felix the other way. It wasn't right for him to kiss me, then ignore me without an explanation. A kiss meant something.

I cut in front of him. "Felix."

"I'm a little busy, Masi," he said. He walked faster. I hurried alongside him. "It's for your own good, Masi. Trust me. It's better this way."

"What is it you're so worried about? No one ever died of a kiss."

"You're wrong. Don't you see this is bigger than a kiss. It's this whole thing, Masi."

"What?"

"Forget it."

"No, you want to say something. So tell me."

"There are things you don't know about. I don't want you thinking Pig Park and *La Gran Pirámide* are anything less than a priority. I like you, but…"

"You don't like me enough. Or you changed your mind."

"That's not it at all. We're just getting to know each other that way. Things were different when I first got here, the first time I kissed you. Now, when the Old Goat screws everyone over—when he does, you're going to hate him. You're going to hate Belinda. And… you're going to hate me. I'm not them, but you're going to hate me anyway, and then we'll both be sorry."

"What do you mean when he screws us over?"

"Look, Belinda told me some things. I didn't want to believe them, but the more I care about you, the more I can't ignore it."

"What are you talking about?"

He took a deep breath. "You know the Xochimilco of Minnesota? They got their visitors eventually. By then the businesses had lost so much that they never recovered. Developers came in and bought up the buildings when the original business owners couldn't afford to pay their taxes. They turned everything into condos, and hardly anyone weathered the storm. That's why the Old Goat buys the buildings, three in Pig Park so far. That's where the profit is."

"When did she tell you?"

"She started telling me one night, but I wouldn't listen. I should've known from the beginning. He isn't a good man. He's a devil."

"You mean figuratively."

"Semantics."

"I don't understand."

"I could grow horns and a tail, and you still wouldn't understand. He's got this way of talking people into doing things and making them feel that it's right, like he did with my mom. The point is, things aren't going to turn out the way you or I want them too."

"Have you told anyone else about this?"

"I haven't told anyone. I don't know what we can do at this point. They'll just shoot the messenger."

"So no one knows?"

"Jorge Peregrino knows. He's known from the beginning. He's a signer."

"What do you mean?"

"He's the kind of person who will sign their life away for a buck. Belinda said he owns the building next to the warehouse and a few of the others too. That's why he made sure to push the plan along when people started to waver."

My hands clenched into fists at my sides. "If this is true, we have to do something. Talk to my dad at least. You have to say something."

"It's not that easy. Everyone is going to hate the Old Goat, and they're going to hate me." It dawned on me what Marcos had meant when he said that Felix was not one of us. He was one of them. "Go home, Masi. Just go home," Felix said.

"You go."

He crossed his arms over his chest and walked away. I didn't really want him to go. I wanted for him to take it back. He turned the corner—and nothing. I didn't know what to do. I trudged back to the bakery.

My dad stood by the worktable in the kitchen. Felix was right about one thing. I was ready to hate him. I was absolutely ready. I hated this whole thing as much as I hated my mom leaving. I felt like grabbing a box of eggs, getting on my bicycle and flinging them at Belinda's SUV, at Peregrino's warehouse, and at Felix's head.

I didn't do any of those things. Eggs weren't free.

My dad pushed his hands into the mixing bowl and formed a ball of masa the size of a fat baby. He punched it down. "Let's fire up that new oven," he said. It occurred to me that he was never going to be able to pay my grandparents back. It wasn't like they needed it, but it would be the worst blow to my dad's pride—worse than not paying the bank, if that was possible.

I rubbed at the back of my neck. "That's an awful lot of masa."

"Maybe not enough. It's for the celebration tomorrow. This is big, Masi. The biggest thing we've done. Everyone will be there."

"Dad—" I didn't know how to tell him. What proof did I even have? "Nothing." I was at a loss.

CHAPTER 39

The boys moved the Chamber's folding table and other furniture to a corner of the pyramid. Loretta placed a bright red tablecloth on the table. The neighborhood restaurants put down their trays of tamales, fajitas, sopes, and various side dishes. My dad and I watched Mrs. Sustaita set up jugs of horchata and agua de tamarindo. We laid out our baskets of sweet bread along with all the other food.

Loretta decorated the edges of the table with foot-high marigold centerpieces. Casey and Stacey hung our papel picado from the exposed beams on the ceiling of the pyramid.

There wasn't a pair of frayed jeans or ratty sneakers in the crowd. We complemented the best Tamaulipas and Jalisco had to offer with the finest slacks, finest skirts, finest shoes, and finest smiles.

Marcos sat in one of the chairs. He polished his trumpet and put the brass instrument to his mouth. The

Fernandez brothers picked up their violin and accordion. Together, they played a do wa ditty that reminded me of their days in the American Academy band.

I sat down with my dad and waited.

Marcos and the Fernandez brothers played until they ran out of songs.

The sun beat down from outside as it shifted overhead. Colonel Franco set up two box fans on the floor, but the ice cubes in the drink jugs still melted into a froth.

There was a loud sigh when a man in a three-piece suit finally appeared. It was as if all of Pig Park had been holding its breath.

Peregrino clapped his hands together. "Welcome, Alderman Chavez," he said in a clear voice meant to bridge the distance.

Loretta ran to Chavez' side and snapped a picture.

He was cool and collected despite the layers of clothes and heat. His eyes glanced over the small group. He shook hands all around and greeted Colonel Franco with a pat on the back. "Didn't you invite anyone else to your opening?" Chavez asked.

"We sent out a number of flyers and invitations," Peregrino cut in. The three men engaged in a hushed conversation.

One minute.

Five minutes.

Ten minutes.

No one else arrived.

No one said much. Even Loretta held her tongue. I imagined it was because of Chavez. Colonel Franco limped to the center of the group. "This is a celebration so let's quit with all the long faces," he said. "We are a small bunch, but a good one. Chavez here has just pledged the City of Chicago's support. He's suggesting new lampposts and sidewalks. Now let's dig in!"

"At least Patricia didn't miss much," Loretta said to my dad.

I rolled my eyes. She just couldn't help butting in.

"She wanted to come. She'll be back in time for the beginning of the school year though. Patricia is spending a few more days with Masi's grandparents. But we already bought her bus ticket home," my dad said. I looked at him. Her scheduled return was news to me.

My dad excused himself, and I followed him. I wanted to know about this bus ticket. "I haven't seen Felix. Have you?" he asked first.

"No." I lied and walked away to avoid getting into it about Felix. I didn't want to lie to my dad.

I'd seen Felix slinking in the shadows, trying to

disappear into the walls. I'd also seen him talking to Belinda who stood by the door with a stupid smile. It was hard to miss them. Felix and Belinda stuck out with their regular people clothes in a room full of human piñatas.

I watched Chavez down a glass of horchata, two tamales and a ginger pig before excusing himself.

Mr. Wong cornered Belinda once Chavez was good and gone. "No one came."

Belinda's jaw dropped. She grasped at the air with her hands. "I don't know what to say."

"Well, you better think of something. We gave Dr. Vidales Casal our money. We built this thing. I sold my car. People dug into their mattresses. We made our kids wear your costumes."

"We did everything you asked short of wearing pig suits," I threw in.

"Masi, be respectful," my dad said.

Felix stepped forward from the shadows. "No. They're both just saying what most of you all must feel," he said.

"Things like these don't always take off overnight. There's no need for you to worry. We'll get the word out and try again. We'll have a big Día de los Muertos celebration," Peregrino interrupted. "This afternoon was really more of a dress rehearsal anyway."

Of course, they didn't know that, according to Felix, we didn't have that kind of time. It was my chance to say something, but I didn't. I don't know why. Maybe I figured that Peregrino could always deny all of it. Without backup from Felix, it was my word against his. I kept my mouth shut like the coward I was.

People wanted to believe Peregrino because some of them began to nod. Not everyone though. "This conversation isn't over," Lorreta said and stomped away. Everyone else packed up their things—the leftover food and respective containers—and headed home. "I'll clean up the rest of it," I said to Colonel Franco and grabbed a few paper plates and cups for the trash can.

"Close up when you're done, Masi," he said. I nodded. I blew out the candles. I thought about the not-so-*gran pirámide*—and my dad and everyone else who lived in Pig Park.

I didn't notice Felix had stayed behind too. His hand on my arm made me jump inside my skin. I backed away and looked up straight into his cat eyes.

"I didn't sign up for this. I thought I'd get my school credit and leave. But I'm not a signer. I care. I want to help fix this," he said.

"Then say something with me," I insisted. There was a long pause. He looked down at his feet. I felt a pang.

The way I figured, he'd didn't care about us if he wasn't at least willing to do that. "We don't need any more of your kind of help. Go home, Felix."

"Home is in New Mexico."

"I don't care."

"I'm not just giving up." He looked up, cat eyes ablaze.

I closed my eyes tight as a water faucet until I sensed that he was gone. I sat there like a spineless mute. I didn't know what else to do. I wanted to get up, run away and get lost.

CHAPTER 40

I stumbled into my dad in the dark bakery hallway. He leaned down and pulled his shoes on. "I'm going over to talk to some of the other families," he said. "Lock the door behind me."

He returned within the hour. "We decided everyone should stay close to home base in case any visitors show up. That's all for now. There's time for the rest to work itself out," he said.

Maybe Felix had followed my dad, because there he was—pounding at the door with an open fist. My dad reached for the deadbolt. I hurried away to my room.

"Can I talk to Masi?" Felix asked, his voice carrying up the stairs.

"Masi?" My dad called out. "She was right here a minute ago. She must've gone to her room. Masi? I'm not sure what's gotten into her."

"It's okay. I wanted to talk to you too. I'm sorry for what happened today. I know you must be worried. I'm going to do everything I can to help. I just wanted you and Masi to know that."

"Don't stress yourself about it. We'll figure something out. You'll see."

I listened to Felix say goodnight and walked back downstairs as soon as I heard the door close.

"Are you angry at Felix?" my dad asked.

"Yes."

"He's a good boy, Masi. I trust that today was not his fault. There's no reason to be angry at him." Of course, my dad didn't know the whole story.

There'd been an incident with rollerblades when I was a kid. I'd tripped on a branch and splattered across hard gravel. Glass on the ground from a nearby broken bottle had buried itself deep into my arm. There'd been a dramatic visit to the hospital with my mom. I'd just wanted not to have to look at all those layers of underskin and blood. I'd been happy for the quick stitches until the bandages came off, and my fingernails dug up glass every time I scratched. Then I wished they'd taken just a little bit more time.

This was like that.

I didn't know Felix at all. Never mind the days we'd spent together or the hours I'd spent watching him with my dad. I'd never really taken the time to know him.

Just like the pyramid, I'd been more in love with who I wanted him to be than who he actually was. Now I was digging up glass. Even worse, I had sold out Pig Park for a pretty face. At least the others had done it for the promise of a better tomorrow.

I sat in front of the TV and stared at the images until I couldn't stand it anymore. I wanted to muster up a Loretta-sized voice and run up and down Pig Park yelling the truth. I pulled out my bike and rode over to Josefina's.

I pushed the bike against the wall into Mrs. Nowak's tomato bushes. Marcos opened the door. One hand held the door knob. The other held a bag of chips. "Masi, what a surprise. You came all this way just to see us."

"Stop messing around. I live down the street," I said.

"Really, I thought you'd moved away. I mean you haven't been by in weeks."

He was right. Josefina stuck her head out from behind him. Marcos stepped around her and slipped back into the grocery store. "You dumped us for Felix," she said.

"I'm sorry." I followed her to her room.

"You better be."

"I am. I won't be wasting any more time on Felix either."

She looked like I'd just given her dog poop and told her it was chocolate. "You mean because he'll be leaving soon? So now you want us back."

"It's not like that. I didn't mean to forget about you. I didn't mean to forget my friends. I was confused by him," I confessed.

"Me and Marcos tried to warn you about him."

"Please don't bring Marcos into this."

"Why not? He hates Felix. And you know about his feelings for you. They are not very brotherly. I always thought we'd end up being real sisters one day."

"Don't say that." How could I tell her that I felt I might lose her, even after everything? And all Marcos ever did was tease me.

"Fine, fine. Just think about something else."

I closed my eyes. I tried to picture Marcos flipping his hair behind his ears. I even flashed back to that fifth-grade kiss. It was the same old el cucuy tactic. But it didn't work.

After Josefina's boyfriend had moved away the previous year, she'd stopped eating for a month. She'd lost ten pounds. After my mom had left my dad, he'd moped around, then gone crazy. He'd nearly buried the house with bread. I didn't want to go crazy. That seemed like a luxury. Someone still needed to save Pig Park or I would lose Josefina and Marcos for real.

I looked at Josefina, tried to look into her. "There's more, but it's getting late," I said.

"I'll walk you out."

Josefina and I stood by the front steps. I don't know how, but I told her all the terrible things I knew. "Why didn't you say anything at the unveiling?" she asked.

"I don't know. I wanted to. It wasn't easy. Remember when we learned about the Spanish conquest of the Americas in history class? We read that essay that talked about how the Aztec rulers accepted defeat as their fate. Maybe this is our fate. Maybe I'm like the ancient Aztecs after all. Maybe Felix and I are not so different. Maybe I am not so different from my mom who ran away either," I said.

"Your mom is trying to fix things. She's coming back."

"You're right." I stared out into the park for a long time. I didn't have to accept this. I opened my mouth and closed it. I sighed and spoke. "But I don't know what to do. What if no one believes me?"

"We'll think of something."

I nodded. Not thinking of something meant the end of Josefina and me. "We'll still be friends, even if the earth swallows up Pig Park, won't we? We'll write, call, text, send smoke signals. Won't we?" I asked. Maybe our friendship was strong enough. It had to be. It had survived a decade of firsts: first days of school, first honor rolls, first periods, first first kisses, first loves, first heartbreaks.

"Yes. We'll still be friends. Best friends," she said. It was exactly what I need to hear. I hugged her and felt a little better. I turned around and walked home.

CHAPTER 41

Loretta sauntered out of the bakery, pulling the door closed behind her. She smoothed her blouse over her thick waist and looked up to see me. I wasn't in the mood to talk. I walked past her.

"Masi, what's wrong?" she asked.

I was done feeding her addiction to gossip. I rubbed my eyes and didn't say anything.

"Masi?" she repeated.

"Don't you already know? Don't you know EVERYTHING? Why didn't you know?" I exploded. Tears rolled down my face. I threw my face into my hands and sobbed.

"Don't cry, mija," she said.

She put her hand on my shoulder. I looked up at her and shook her off like fire. "I'm not your mija," I said.

I knew then that the tears weren't just about losing my friends or Felix or Pig Park. I needed my mom. I needed her advice. I needed for her to be the one asking me if I was okay. I needed it to be her hand on my shoulder. I missed her as much as my dad did.

"I know I'm not your mom, Masi. But your mother and I both grew up here in Pig Park. She's my oldest friend. I promised her I would look after you and your dad. I'm going to keep an eye on you no matter who hates it."

"I miss her."

"We all miss her. Go inside and call her. You'll feel better."

"I'm sorry." My shoulders sagged with shame.

"Nothing to feel sorry about. I would walk on nails for your mother. Go on inside now."

I walked inside. I picked up the phone and dialed my grandmother's number. "Mom?"

"Masi. I've called the house several times. No one answers."

"I'm sorry, Mom. I miss you. I want you to come home. There, I said it."

"I miss you too. And, I am coming home. I'm sorry you got caught in the middle of this. I love you."

"You promise?"

"Yes. I love you. Get some rest, Masi. It's late. We'll talk later." I put the phone back in its place and went to bed.

I stared at the ceiling. It dawned on me that Loretta

and my mom were not that different from Josefina and me. Though I had a hard time imagining that they were ever young. I pictured Loretta, age fifteen, wearing rollers as she walked to school with my mom. A smile tugged at the corners of my mouth.

My mom and Josefina were the type to walk away. Loretta and I were the type to care a little too much sometimes. Loretta was just trying to hold on, like me. She knew everything because my mom had asked her to look out for us. My mom talked to her. They kept each other in the loop. That meant my mom cared too. Physical distance didn't make a person stop caring.

I tried to focus on what mattered and numb any selfish thing inside me.

I ran upstairs and threw myself on my bed. I knew I had to clear my mind if I wanted to figure anything out. I did what Josefina suggested. I pushed Felix out. I grasped for other thoughts and tried not to scratch at what Felix had left behind. Felix could leave—and he would leave and never come back. But Pig Park was home to the rest of us.

I can't say that I prayed, but it was something like it. Mostly, I wished for a miracle to save us. If a wish had brought Felix here, then maybe it could fix this. *Please, please, please.* I wanted Felix to be wrong.

I tiptoed into the living room and picked up the phone again. "Josefina, let's call all our friends and have them meet us at the park tomorrow morning. I'm going to tell them everything I know, and we're going to figure this out together."

CHAPTER 42

There was a loud bang and something like the soft roll of thunder. The phone rang. I stumbled out into the hallway. My dad hung the receiver up on its holster. His hands closed around my shoulders. He looked into my face.

"Listen carefully. That was Loretta. There's been an explosion. We have to leave right now."

"An explosion?" It was the middle of the night. Was I dreaming, or was good old Loretta finally making good on that promise of watching out for us?

"At the park. Grab your shoes."

I slipped on my sneakers, not bothering with socks, and followed my dad into the street. My eyes opened wide. Fire licked at the pyramid like ten giant tongues lapping it up. It roared.

"Run!" my dad yelled.

Every sound of my body was magnified.

Every breath.

Every slap of rubber soles against the ground.

We ran past the park. We ran to the American Lard Company's north parking lot just as if it were written in a manual. It was the biggest open space away from the buildings and all their flammable parts.

Loretta counted to make sure everyone was safe: Peregrino, Felix, Father Arturo, the Burciagas, the Nowaks, the Wongs, the Fernandez, Sanchez and Sustaita families. Colonel Franco limped in at the tail end.

"I don't know about the rest of you, but I'm not one to stand here and watch the whole neighborhood go up in flames," Colonel Franco said. He bounced from side to side on his good leg. He was an old pitbull ready to pounce.

"I called the fire department," Loretta said.

"The entire neighborhood will go up by the time they get here. Let's head over there and see if we can do something now."

"Yes, they'll probably need help getting in with those big fire trucks," my dad said.

"You go," Loretta cornered us even further away from the fire like a big mother hen. "The girls and I will stay here where it's safe."

"She's right. You go ahead. I'll stay with them and

make sure everyone is safe," Peregrino said— out to protect his own hide. I narrowed my eyes at him.

Father Arturo dropped to his knees. He put his face to the pavement and clasped his hands together on top of his head. "Our father who art in Heaven/ hallowed be thy name..." He mumbled his prayers into the earth.

The men and boys, with the exception of Peregrino and Father Arturo, marched into a cloud of smoke that billowed and grew. I broke away from Loretta and trudged into the cloud after them. I heard a second set of footsteps and turned around. Josefina followed close behind.

Smoke stung my eyes and my lungs. It wasn't the same dizzying smokiness that once drew me to Felix. It smelled of pork rinds. My belly rumbled—or maybe it was a building coming down. I closed my eyes. I held them shut for a second. I opened them. The others disappeared.

"Do you see them?"

"No." Josefina's voice quivered. "Masi, I hope they're okay."

I grabbed her hand. I covered my nose and mouth with my free hand and squinted. Belinda's dumpster lay on its side halfway across the park. There were wires and scorched drywall everywhere. The bakery's old oven sat in the middle of the street like it'd fallen out of the sky. The pyramid had burned to a crumble of brick and cinder so that only the metal beams remained erect.

The fire wasn't done. It lapped at Belinda and Peregrino's buildings. It inched toward the old school building.

Josefina squeezed my hand. She pointed to a group of silhouettes by the train tracks. There were muffled voices. The men had gone around the west side of the park.

Sirens sounded and flashing lights struggled through the smoke. I couldn't help but sigh.

"Let's get over there," I said.

"We'll have to go all the way back and around."

I pushed my face into the inside of my elbow. We walked in a circle. The muffled voices tried to direct the trucks in, but the trucks didn't seem able to work their way around. American Academy folded to its knees. The firemen took a wrench to the closest hydrant and unraveled the length of their hoses. They screwed two nozzles together to reach the flames from the outside. Water gushed into the air.

Time stampeded, and the storm finally turned the tormenter to embers.

The smoke parted like a curtain, revealing a crowd of

strangers on the other side. The commotion had woken up people in the adjacent neighborhoods. They stood there in their pajamas rubbing the eye snot from their faces.

"There's nothing to see here," said a big red-bearded fireman. He stood tall and in charge. "Go on home, the fire is contained."

A few groans followed, but the crowd dispersed back into the shadows. The Pig Park men walked back around the cinder, puddles, and muck toward the fire truck. Josefina ran to Mr. Nowak and threw her arms around him like she was never letting go.

Colonel Franco addressed the red-bearded firefighter. "What happened? Can you tell us anything?"

"It looks like it started in that dumpster. There will be an official investigation, but it doesn't look intentional. Something someone threw away probably. Some kind of reaction," he said.

Reaction? That was chemistry talk.

My dad's face was darkened by smoke and fatigue. Felix, on the other hand, was all teeth. I walked up to him and whispered. "Did you have something to do with this? Did you set that fire?" It wasn't bad enough about everything else. He'd turned arsonist and criminal.

"Shh, I'm trying to listen."

"Someone could've gotten hurt."

"Everyone is fine."

"There is quite a bit of property damage," the fireman said. His men packed up the hoses.

"Well, we're just glad everyone's okay. We are very grateful to you." My dad extended his hand. He moved from firefighter to firefighter wrapping their palms into his. The group followed suit.

The firefighters loaded into the truck and backed up out of Pig Park, their exit having been made easier by the devastation of several buildings.

"I guess that's that," Mr. Nowak said.

"We'll see what tomorrow brings," my dad said. "I hope this doesn't affect your grade, Felix." My dad patted Felix on the back. Felix smiled even wider.

Everyone broke off in their respective directions. My dad and I slumped home. He put his arm around my shoulder. "Everyone's safe, that's all that matters. Oh, and let's not worry your mom with this business of the fire. We don't want her blood sugar going up," he said.

"Okay." I was too exhausted to voice an opinion. I didn't even bother washing off the soot and smell of pork rinds. I didn't give Felix a single additional thought. I dropped on the couch and sat there until the nightmare turned to darkness.

CHAPTER 43

It wasn't a dream. People trickled in to behold the devastation. They arrived walking, on the train and in cars. The fire had left a gaping hole, and opened Pig Park like a giant wound for everyone to stare at.

The alien faces trekked in cautiously. They stuck close to the park and what could best be described as the pyramid ruins. They weren't exactly the kind of visitors we were promised, but it was something.

"What now?" I asked my dad

"We start again. We rise from the ashes." He was right. Pig Park had seen worse.

Everything else went back to normal. It was like the pyramid had never existed. My dad baked. I scrubbed the kitchen clean and manned the counter.

"Dad. Maybe we can cut up some bread into tiny squares and put them out as samples for the people out there." I pointed toward the train stop. "If people like it, they'll buy the bread from us."

"Sure. We can give it a try. Your mom put out samples of bread every morning when we first got married," he said. I smiled. It was nice to learn something new about her. She had really cared about this place once. Maybe she could again.

I took a large permanent marker and wrote 'free taste samples' on a piece of paper. I taped it to the door. I cut up a couple of ginger pigs into two-inch squares and set them on a tray with a folded card that read 'try.' I waited for people to come. No one ventured further than the park. I picked at the ginger pig squares. I rose, and headed out into the park with my tray.

I stumbled into a lady carrying a legal pad just outside the door. "Hi there," she said. "Nice shirt."

I looked down and smoothed out my fuchsia shirt. "Thanks. It's kind of my uniform." I didn't have to wear it now that the pyramid was gone, but I didn't mind so much anymore. I was running out of clean clothes again.

I held the door open for her. "Come in."

"My name is Wendy Jones."

"Do you live on the other side? I mean, on the other side of the tracks."

"I live over by Eastside High. I teach there too." Eastside was the big school one mile east of Pig Park.

"I'm Masi."

"I looked up at the sky and noticed the tip of your pyramid sticking out above the trees a couple of days ago when I was setting up my classroom. I drove in this morning and saw immediately that something had happened. The popsicle man that rides by after school every day told me about the fire. I got curious. I didn't even know there were people still living back here," she said.

"There's still a few of us out here. The American Lard Company's buildings just blocked us from everyone until they burned down." I paused. Our school situation had suffered the worst of it. There was no going back for sure now. "Our school was one of the other buildings that burned down. They'd closed it down at the end of spring. They're busing us to Eastside this fall. I'll be a sophomore."

"I teach junior English. Maybe you'll be in one of my classes in a couple of years."

She smiled. She was nice enough. If Eastside had more teachers like her then maybe it didn't matter that American Academy was gone for good.

"Would you like to try some bread?" I asked.

"Yes, I was walking around, and I saw your sign. I thought, why not? This could be an adventure." Mrs. Jones grabbed a sample and put it in her mouth. I studied her as her lips curved with approval. Her smile broadened with genuine gusto. "These are absolutely fantastic!"

"Everything is made fresh daily," I said.

"What are they called?" she asked.

"Ginger pigs or *marranitos*. There's no ginger in the recipe. The name is a reference to the color."

"Ginger or no ginger, give me a couple of them," she said. I put on a glove and dropped a pair of ginger pigs in a paper bag. She handed me a five-dollar bill, and I rang her up. "This can't be good for my diet."

"We make a healthy version too. It tastes just the same, but we don't have any today. We call them Skinny Pigs. Here's our phone number. If you give us a head's up, my dad can bake them to order. Then you can also visit some of the other businesses while you're here."

"Oh, I'd love that. You certainly haven't seen the last of me. I have a big mouth. Good for eating—and also good for telling everyone I know about this place," she said.

I saw her to the door and hung up the Closed sign. I wiped down the counters. The phone rang.

"Masi? This is Mrs. Jones. My husband and I'd like to come back tomorrow to try some of that special order bread."

"That's great. I'll let me dad know." I ran upstairs. I couldn't wait to tell my dad how well my sample idea had worked out.

CHAPTER 44

"The wet ingredients are ready," I said. My dad rolled up his sleeves. He sifted together the shortening, baking soda, and cinnamon. He poured in the vanilla, yacón syrup, egg and milk mixture. He added the flour, mixed it all until it came together and rolled out the masa. I pressed down with the pig-shaped cookie cutters. I peeled off the cuttings and laid out the pigs on a baking sheet. My dad brushed them with the egg wash and popped them into the oven.

The smell of butter and cinnamon escaped into the air after a few minutes. I peeked through the fancy new oven's window and watched as the pigs plumped under the heat.

"Set them out to cool and put them in the display case with the rest of the bread I made this morning when they're done," my dad said. He took off his apron.

"Where are you going?" I asked.

"Upstairs."

"Don't you want to meet them?"

"This is your show."

My dad disappeared. I took out the bread and slid the tray into the rack for them to cool. I sorted the junk mail. It was all I could do to keep myself from breaking a ginger pig in half and inhaling it. An hour passed before the Joneses arrived. I ran to the door and held it open for them. "This is my husband," Mrs. Jones said. The mustached man in shorts and a baseball cap grabbed my hand and shook it.

"What is that?" He pointed to the window.

"It's an altar for the Day of the Dead. All of the Pig Park businesses set them up before the fire. This particular altar is for my abuelita Carmelita who started this bakery with my dad." I walked to the window and picked up the picture of her. "Day of the Dead is like All Souls Day. Every year at the beginning of November, people celebrate their loved ones who have died. They go to cemeteries with flowers, candles, food and music. They also put up altars at home for them."

"Very interesting," Mr. Jones said.

"Masi is going to be a student at Eastside next year. Maybe she can get a Day of the Dead celebration going there. She can bring in some bread," Mrs. Jones said to him. She winked at me. I liked her more and more.

"Is this your summer job?" Mr. Jones asked.

"Something like that. It's a family business. All of the businesses in Pig Park are family businesses."

"So tell me about this array you have here."

I told Mr. Jones all about the *conchas, cuernitos, bolillos* and *marranitos.* "Try some. The bread will speak for itself," I said, remembering something my dad had said to Felix an eternity ago.

Mr. Jones bit into a ginger pig. He closed his eyes when he bit down and savored each bite. "Give me a dozen each of whatever you have, in addition to my wife's order. I'm taking these to work later this afternoon," he said.

It was everything we had. I put on a glove and threw the bread in a paper bag. It was more than we'd sold all summer. I took off the glove and rung the order up. Mr. Jones handed me three twenty-dollar bills. I gave him his change and the Joneses headed out. "Thank you so much. I hope you'll come again, or maybe I'll see you at school." I waved goodbye.

I locked the front door and ran upstairs. "Can we close early? There's nothing left," I said. The corners of my mouth pushed against my cheeks like my face was gonna split in two.

"Nothing?"

"Yes."

"I should have you working sales exclusively from now on."

"Just luck. So can we close?"

"No. Someone else might still walk in and place an order," he said.

I sat by the counter all day. No else walked in, but it didn't matter. *Rise from the ashes*, that's what my dad had said. Or maybe from the bread crumbs.

CHAPTER 45

"It's all worked out, Tomás. The investigator ruled that the fire started in the dumpster, probably with your old oven," Peregrino said.

"My oven?" My dad's mouth dropped.

"And some drywall, and a cigarette someone threw in there. But it wasn't your fault. It was the Lard Company's improper disposal of their highly flammable waste that allowed it to spread. My attorney spent a few hours on the phone with their insurance company last night. They're willing to compensate us for our losses at a hundred and fifty percent so long as we sign waivers," Peregrino continued.

My dad let out a deep breath. Peregrino shrugged as if it was no bigger deal than someone changing the packaging of cod liver tablets from green to blue. He was getting a fat check after all, which was all he'd ever wanted according to Felix. Peregrino had enough sources of income that I suppose it didn't matter.

"As the owner of record for *La Gran Pirámide*, the Chamber will do very nicely. Now it's up to the neighborhood to decide if you want to rebuild. I'm off to tell Colonel Franco," Peregrino said and left.

My dad pushed a tray of ginger pigs into the display case and sat at the counter—looking both relieved and astonished. I wiped down the counter in front of him.

Felix walked in with his backpack on and a duffle bag over his shoulder. I leaned into the display case and made myself busy sweeping for crumbs.

"You doing laundry, Felix?" my dad asked.

"I heard you guys are getting your money back. I'm glad. With *La Gran Pirámide* gone and school starting soon, there's nothing left for me to do. I'm heading back home. I just came to say goodbye." Felix extended his hand to my dad.

My dad grabbed Felix's hand and pulled him into a hug. "Keep in touch. We'll miss you, but I'm sure your mom will be glad to have you back." My dad took a plastic bag and threw in some bread. "This is for your trip. Masi, come say goodbye."

I walked over to them. Felix blinked at wet eyes and smiled that beautiful smile.

"You going somewhere?" I asked, as if I hadn't been listening.

"Yes. Home to New Mexico."

"I'll walk you to the train." We walked side by side. It was like we were going downtown again. Except, completely different. There was a heaviness between us. I stopped in front of the platform.

"Masi, there's something I need to clear up before I go," he said.

"You don't have to."

"I really did like you. I made a bad choice that I have to live with," he said. "If it makes you feel any better, they fooled me too. Belinda packed up and left like a thief in the night. No apologies. No goodbyes. She drove away as soon as she heard about the check. She offered me a ride back home, but I wanted to wait until I saw you and your dad. I did everything I could to try to make amends. You can't hate me for that."

"Did you set that fire? Did you?"

"Please don't ask. I'll have to tell you the truth this time." He leaned in and grabbed hold of my wrist. I squirmed, but he tightened his hold. His face came closer and closer. It wasn't magic. It was real. I forgot the question. My eyes shut. My body betrayed me. I jolted out of the kiss. "You can't do that," I said. It was too little too late.

Felix stumbled back. "I'm leaving."

"That doesn't change what happened."

"It means there's no time left for regret."

Train lights approached in the distance. The train screeched to a stop. His voice carried over the train's commotion. "Maybe this isn't the end," he said.

The door folded shut. The boy of a thousand questions disappeared as suddenly as he had appeared. I thought about all the things I almost lost. I thought about my friends, Pig Park and the bakery, and I knew he was wrong. It *was* the end. I felt a little sorry, but he was right about one thing. There was no time left for regret.

CHAPTER 46

I walked into the bakery. Loretta stood by the counter with my dad. A pair of glasses hung from a chain around her neck. The computer sat open in front of her. A newspaper lay spread out on the counter. A dozen copies of the same paper sat off to the side in a stack.

"What's going on?" I asked.

Loretta looked up. "Mija, I called everyone. Your phone was busy. The news just couldn't wait. I had to come in person."

"I was talking to Patricia." My dad blushed. "She was telling me about her doctor's visit."

I panicked. Was he about to tell me my mom wasn't coming back as planned? "Did something happen?" I asked.

"No. Nothing like that. Your grandmother insisted she get a checkup before traveling. The doctor cleared her to head home. In fact, she's all packed. She'll be back by the first day of school for you. We were just confirming the arrangements for her trip," my dad said. I let out a deep breath. "Loretta is here because we're in the newspaper."

"Look at this, Masi. Page thirty-two of the *Times*. Online and printed editions. Ooh, Patricia will be very excited to see this good news," Loretta said. She motioned for me to come closer and moved aside, so I could see.

The headline read: BLAZE REVEALS NEIGHBORHOOD GEM by Bill Jones. *Bill Jones.* "Hey, I think that's Mrs. Jones' husband," I said.

"Mrs. who?" Loretta asked.

"She's the Eastside teacher who came the other day. I sold her and her husband a day's worth of bread. They bought everything we had." I picked up the section and read aloud.

"Located amidst the compound of the recently abandoned American Lard Company, Pig Park is a neighborhood most have never heard of. A five-alarm fire last week revealed that gem of a neighborhood and a definite place to explore. Bypass the steel ruins of their once ambitious pyramid, a modernist replica sculpture built on the southeast side of the park, to treat yourself. The local flower shop offers flowers more fragrant and colorful than any market abroad—great for any occasion—"

"That's me," Loretta laughed.

"Several family restaurants will take you back to mother's kitchen, though not necessarily your own mother—still an excellent homage to homecooking. The bakery will satisfy any sweet tooth. If you think you can't have sweets, try the Skinny Pig. My wife, the health fiend, polished off half a dozen in one afternoon—"

"That's us." My dad blushed a second time.

"Indeed it is." Loretta clapped and nodded. Her eyes scanned the room. "So what's this about a Skinny Pig?"

"It's our latest recipe. A healthier version of our marranito. Masi, give Loretta a taste."

I walked to the kitchen and took the tray of Skinny Pigs from the cooling rack. I passed the tray in front of Loretta. She reached for one, broke off a piece and nibbled on it. She smiled and gobbled the rest down, but didn't say anything. Maybe she was at a loss of words for once.

"So?" my dad asked.

"I can see what the rave is about. Wow. Put a few of these in a bag for me to take home. My girls could stand to eat a little healthier."

I stuffed half a dozen Skinny Pigs into a paper bag

and handed it to her. I smiled. My dad smiled. Loretta smiled.

She took the stack of newspapers with her free hand. She pointed to the paper on the counter I'd read from earlier. "I'm leaving that copy so you can show your mom. I know you can just print it from the computer, but it's not the same. Getting in the printed newspaper, that's the real deal. It won't be gone tomorrow. They can't just hit delete. Mark my words. This is going to change everything. EVERYTHING! Pig Park is on the map now, mija."

Loretta practically danced out the door. Pig Park— that was us. It was the end of summer and nothing would be the same.

CHAPTER 47

I grabbed a copy of the newspaper article and tacked it on the wall. "We should probably clean up for when Mom gets back," I said. We divided up the chores between us. I ran the washer/dryer, folded laundry on the kitchen table, and put the clothes away. My dad dusted the furniture, wiped down the counters, and ran the vacuum in the living room.

We worked all night. I didn't care that the next day was the first day of school. I couldn't sleep anyway. I showered and dressed. My dad came out of his room fidgeting with the collar of his white dress shirt.

I heard footsteps on the stairs. I ran to the door and opened it. My mom stepped through. My dad's eyes lit up. He stepped forward. He was a young man again, watching his dream girl stroll across a room. "Once I thought I lost the girl I loved, but she came back," he murmured. He grabbed her so tenderly that I was forced to look away.

"Masi, come," he said. He pulled me in with them.

My mom's arm wrapped around me. "I'm sorry," she said. I grabbed her tight.

"Give me a second," my dad said and disappeared. I pulled my mom's bag into her room and began unpacking for her.

"I'm never leaving again. I blamed your dad and the bakery for how I felt. But I wasn't myself. I want you to know that. I love you, Masi," she said. She hugged me a second time. We stood like that for an eternity. Her arms were an eraser. It was almost like she had never left, except that her leaving and getting sick had resulted in my dad's creation of the Skinny Pig.

"You were sick, Mom."

"I have your surprise," my dad said from the hallway. He walked into the room with a dozen Skinny Pigs on a tray.

"What's this?" my mom asked.

"Skinny Pigs. Sugarfree for your diabetes," I said. I broke away and grabbed the copy of the newspaper article. I handed it to her.

She bit into a Skinny Pig as she read. Her mouth blossomed into a smile. "So that's what happened out there," she said.

"We have a lot to talk about," my dad said. Of course, she had seen all the burnt-down buildings and the new faces coming off the trains. The pyramid scheme had led Felix here, sparked the fire and brought down the American Lard buildings so people would notice us. It had brought Mr. Jones here to write that article so that, from one night to the next, there'd been visitors from all over the city straying beyond the park. But it was the Skinny Pigs that kept people coming back to the bakery. We had our hands full. They were now our biggest seller. Things weren't perfect, but they were getting better.

"No more letters from the bank," I said. I ran back to my room to get my backpack. I heard the sound of dresser drawers being knocked around in their room. Or maybe something else. There was giggling. The knocking stopped. I rolled my eyes and laughed.

"I'm going to school now," I yelled as if they weren't otherwise occupied. I slipped on the backpack and walked past the train tracks toward the new school bus stop. Josefina waved. Marcos angled his head. His bangs fell away from his eyes. The richness of their brown popped off his face.

Marcos grabbed my bag. I smiled. He smiled. His cheeks dimpled. He winked. I thought about what Josefina had said and flashed back to that 5th grade kiss. The heat rose up my spine. I had no trouble wrapping my head around it. "I'm ready," I said.

ACKNOWLEDGMENTS

I am grateful to Lou, Penny and the baby for teaching me that the world is an ever-evolving place: I live in a world full of people. Gracias a mi mamá, Concha, y mis hermanos(as) por su paciencia. Thank you to Alicia and Susana for being bookworms.

I am also grateful to Lee Byrd for not tossing that first draft of *The Smell of Old Lady Perfume* into the recycling bin and helping me to become a better writer with every draft. Thank you also to my Prairie Writers Critique Group—Mary Joe Guglielmo, Jane Hertenstein, and Tim Brandhorst—for your encouragement and expertise. A special thanks to the Illinois Arts Council Individual Artist Support Initiative and the City of Chicago Community Arts Assistance Program for their support of my development as a writer.

Finally, thanks to everyone, mentioned and not mentioned, who stood with me in the Pig Park of my imagination and watched that crazy pyramid get built!